"I have a question for you. You had arranged to pick me up at five o'clock, in just a few hours, for a date. Doesn't it seem weird for you to ring the doorbell and announce that you're moving in with me?"

"A valid question." He translated her concern: "You want to know if it's unprofessional for me to agree to act as bodyguard for a woman I'm attracted to."

"Are you?" She brightened.

"Attracted?" He regretted the use of that word. "You're a good-looking woman. I'm a single man."

"And you're my bodyguard. If we're dating, isn't that a professional conflict?"

"I considered asking somebody else at TST to take this assignment." For about three and a half seconds, he'd considered. "It's not a problem. I can control my personal feelings. At five o'clock, I can quit being a bodyguard, and we'll have our date. Or not."

"How do you decide?"

"We'll know," he said.

MOUNTAIN BODYGUARD

USA TODAY Bestselling Author
CASSIE MILES

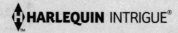

HARLEQUIN INTRIGUE®

To Khloe Adams and her brilliant advice. And, as always, to Rick.

Recycling programs
for this product may
not exist in your area.

ISBN-13: 978-0-373-69918-6

Mountain Bodyguard

Copyright © 2016 by Kay Bergstrom

Printed in U.S.A.

www.Harlequin.com

Cassie Miles a *USA TODAY* bestselling author, lives in Colorado. After raising two daughters and cooking tons of macaroni and cheese for her family, Cassie is trying to be more adventurous in her culinary efforts. She's discovered that almost anything tastes better with wine. When she's not plotting Harlequin Intrigue books, Cassie likes to hang out at the Denver Botanical Gardens near her high-rise home.

Books by Cassie Miles

Harlequin Intrigue

Mountain Midwife
Sovereign Sheriff
Baby Battalion
Unforgettable
Midwife Cover
Mommy Midwife
Montana Midwife
Hostage Midwife
Mountain Heiress
Snowed In
Snow Blind
Mountain Retreat
Colorado Wildfire
Mountain Bodyguard

CAST OF CHARACTERS

Francine Alexandra DeMille, aka Lexie DeMille, aka Franny DeMille—After sustaining serious injuries in a car accident, the rough-and-tumble tomboy takes a job as a nanny for six children.

Mason Steele—Part owner of TST Security, based in Denver, he faces an intense challenge: protecting Lexie.

Sean and Dylan Timmons—The other two partners in TST.

Admiral Edgar Prescott—Though retired from navy intelligence operations, his expertise is valued in the spy community.

Helena Christie Prescott—Second wife of the admiral; she's a fabulous movie star.

Prescott children—Meggie and Eddie Jr. are teenagers. The twins (age ten) are Caine and Shane. Todd is six. Stella is four.

Daniel DeMille—Lexie's father is retired from the marines.

Anton Karpov, aka Tony Curtis—Lexie's former boyfriend who failed at his first chance to kill her and wants to try again.

Al Ackerman—Deceased agent, he was the last to see the Damascus Cache.

Josh Laurent—An assistant for Prescott with a hidden agenda.

Hank Grossman—Works at the NSA and suspects everyone.

Sam Bertinelli—Disgruntled junior NSA agent who resents reporting to Grossman.

Robert Collier—Dashing CIA agent who knows more than anyone else.

Chapter One

The hotel was a bodyguard's nightmare. Mason Steele fidgeted beside French doors that opened onto a flag-stone terrace. With extreme impatience, he watched while Admiral Edgar Prescott, tonight's honoree, made his way through the stragglers who were toasting the crimson glow of a June sunset and finishing off their complementary glass of Colorado merlot.

Number one security problem: isolated mountain location. This seven-story structure was surrounded by national forest with only two viable access roads. Never mind that Aspen was less than forty minutes away, this site was remote. An attacker could assault the hotel, dash across the ninth green and vanish into the forest before Mason and his colleagues figured out where they were hit. To prevent such an ambush, his firm, TST Security, had stationed their own snipers on the roof.

This charity banquet was all hands on deck for TST. They were using five regulars and six part-timers, plus had a helicopter pilot on standby.

Security issue number two: though the styling of the

hotel was meant to resemble a hunting lodge from the early 1900s, the interior of the banquet hall featured a wall of windows and another of French doors. The design was an open invitation to long-distance shooters.

Issue number three: the people. Too many had been invited. The circular tables reached almost to the walls, which meant a sure pileup if they had to evacuate quickly. The well-dressed guests had all passed through metal detectors, but that was no guarantee of safety in this era of plastic firearms. Potential weapons were everywhere. Prime rib was on the menu; steak knives were on the tables. The centerpieces blocked sight lines, and the tall Art Deco arrangements on either side of the dais were large enough to hide a couple of AK-47s.

As soon as the admiral stepped over the threshold from the terrace, Mason signaled to one of his men to round up the last few people that were outside and lock the French doors. As for himself, he took a position against the wall where he could watch the crowd. Most of them had settled into their assigned seats. Some had already been served. Others table hopped, chatted and chuckled and showed off photos on cell phones.

A woman in a sleeveless blue jumpsuit approached him. He'd been introduced to her before, had noticed her thoroughly and had paid particular attention to the way the clingy blue fabric hugged her curves. She was part of the entourage for the admiral, his movie star wife and their several children. When the lady in blue sidled up next to him, the top of her head was only as high as his shoulder. Lights from the chandeliers glistened on her curly auburn ponytail.

She nudged his elbow. "Whose body are you guarding?"

"The admiral's." He dropped a glance in her direction, expecting to quickly look away. Instead, she seized his attention with her big brown eyes and the constellation of freckles that spread across her nose and cheeks. The corners of her mouth naturally turned upward as though caught on the edge of laughter.

"Your friend across the room," she said with a nod toward Sean Timmons, who was the first *T* in TST Security, "must be in charge of watching Helena Christie Prescott's body. How did he get the good assignment?"

"Seniority." The admiral's glamorous dark-haired wife showed a lot of cleavage, and the slit on her skirt was thigh high. Watching her was kind of a treat.

"You're Mason, right?"

"Yes, ma'am." Mason Steele was the *S* in TST Security. "And you're Francine Alexandra DeMille."

"Call me Lexie."

"Why not Francine?" he asked. "Or Franny?"

"Because of my job. I take care of the Prescott kids."

Which made her Franny the nanny? He stifled a chuckle. "There are six of them, right?"

"Two teenagers from the admiral's first marriage. The ten-year-old twin boys come from Helena's union with the hunk who's in that stripper movie—a deadbeat dad, but, oh, those abs."

"I know who you mean."

She stared intently at him. "You look a little bit like him. With the buzz haircut and the cool blue eyes and those big, muscular…arms." She squeezed one of his biceps and immediately yanked her hand away. A pink blush colored her cheeks. "And the six- and four-year-old are from this marriage."

When he forced his gaze away from her and checked out the children's table, the littlest girl stood up on the seat of her chair and waved at him with a golden magic wand. He fought the urge to laugh. On the job, he couldn't afford to be distracted by cuteness, but this little golden-haired girl was irresistible. He grinned back at her and winked.

Mason had always thought a big family would be fun. He was his parents' only surviving child. Thanksgiving was no picnic. And Christmas? Forget about it.

"Here's my problem," Lexie said. "The younger kiddos are restless and on the verge of turning into a nuisance. The older ones are bored. And we're at least a half hour away from the speeches. Do you have any security issues if I whisk them out of here in a few minutes?"

He was glad she'd asked before dashing out the door. TST provided extra security when children were part of the scene. Mason looked around the banquet room, trying to spot the bodyguard who was responsible for keeping an eye on the Prescott offspring.

"Strange," he muttered. "I don't see Carlos."

"Nope." Lexie shook her head, and her curly ponytail bounced. "He introduced himself earlier, and I would have gone to him, but I lost track of where he was, which is kind of hard to do, since good old Carlos is the size of a side-by-side refrigerator-freezer combo."

A former pro football linebacker, Carlos was six feet five inches—only a little taller than Mason, but Carlos outweighed him by nearly seventy-five pounds. The big man was good at his job and wasn't the type to wander off.

Where the hell was he? A twang of apprehension jangled Mason's nerves. "It might be a good idea to get the kids out of here."

Immediately, Lexie picked up on his mood. Her grin disappeared. "Is it dangerous?"

Always. There was always danger. He didn't want to tell her that; didn't want to point out the obvious fact that his security firm had been hired to protect the admiral and his family from an imminent threat, which meant a threat existed.

"Let's see what I can find out." He gave her a light pat on the shoulder. His intention had been to reassure her, but when he touched her bare skin, a spark ignited. Like wildfire, an unexpected heat crackled though his nerve endings and turned his blood to lava. For an instant, he was struck dumb. He had to drag his focus away from Lexie before he spoke into his headset to Sean.

After a quick, quiet conversation with his partner, Mason regained his self-control. There was no room for further distraction; tonight was important. TST was there to protect Admiral Prescott, a man he respected and admired. Though the admiral had been retired for three years and wasn't in uniform tonight, his posture bespoke military discipline. Mason's brother, an expert in naval intelligence, had known the admiral personally.

Lexie cleared her throat. She looked to him for an

all-clear signal. He wanted to give her a thumbs-up so she'd reward him with that cute upturned smile of hers. When she lifted her hand to brush back a wisp of russet hair, he noticed her delicate charm bracelet. The silver chain shone brightly against her tanned forearm. One of the charms resembled a ninja throwing star.

Sean's voice came through his earbud. "I found Carlos. I knew I'd seen the big guy headed this way. He's in the bathroom, puking his guts out."

"What's wrong with him?"

"Might have the flu," Sean said. "One of his kids is sick."

Or he could have been drugged, could have been poisoned. Several scenarios flipped through Mason's mind, ranging from an attempted abduction of the children to a full-on assault with fiery explosive devices. In every possible circumstance, he needed to get the children to safety.

Keeping his voice calm, he spoke to Lexie. "Tell the kids we're leaving. We'll go out through the terrace. It's the closest exit."

"Should I be worried?"

Not wanting to alarm her, he didn't offer an explanation. "I thought you wanted to get the kids away."

"True, and I don't mind missing those speeches myself."

With a toss of her head, she pivoted and returned to the circular table where the Prescott brood was sitting. The teenagers were texting, the younger kids were playing with their food and the princess with the magic wand was waving to everyone.

In a hushed tone, Mason informed Sean that he'd take over Carlos's job, guarding the children and moving them upstairs to their bedrooms. The hotel had provided extra security guards on the seventh floor, where the entourage was staying. "While I'm gone, you watch the admiral."

"I'm worried," Sean said. "What if Carlos was drugged?"

Mason was about to ask if Carlos had eaten anything or had anything to drink. Before he spoke, he realized that it was a dumb question. Carlos was always eating and drinking. "Let's hope it's just the flu."

He scanned the crowd. As more people were served, the sound of conversation was replaced by the clink of silverware against china. The situation was under control. Earlier today, they'd come up with several possible evacuation plans. But what if the attackers had outthought them and were already waiting outside? Mason contacted his snipers on the roof, letting them know that he intended to exit with the kids.

He seriously doubted that the bad guys had gained entrance to the banquet hall. The guests, cooks and servers had all been vetted and the TST Security computers were a foolproof system, protected by something Dylan Timmons, who was the second *T* in TST Security, called the mother of all firewalls.

Mason's gaze flicked around the room. Could he trust computer clearances? Doubt assailed his judgment. "Maybe we should shut this operation down."

A voice in his head—which was actually Sean—advised, "It's your call, Mason."

At TST Security, the three partners had their areas of expertise. Dylan specialized in computer security. Sean was former FBI, more of a detective and a profiler—a deductive genius. And Mason was the muscle—the man in charge of action and strategy. "First, I'll get the kids to safety."

As if he needed another complication, the admiral had left his banquet seat and was coming toward him. Smiling and genial, the admiral picked his way through the crowd and stood beside Mason. "What's the problem?"

"The bodyguard protecting the children has a suspicious case of the flu." He kept his voice low so the other guests wouldn't take notice. "It's probably nothing, but I recommend escorting the kids to their rooms on the seventh floor."

"Agreed. I don't take chances with my children's safety." He beckoned to Lexie, who began moving the kids in their direction. "I'll help."

"My men can handle the situation, Admiral. It's not necessary for you to leave the banquet."

"I'm retired, Mr. Steele. You can drop the admiral and call me Prescott. But make no mistake—I still give the orders."

The expression on Mason's face didn't change a bit. Inside, he was cheering for the old warrior who was still man enough to take care of his children, marry a movie star and lead the charge into battle. Still, he said, "Sir, let me do my job. If you come, I need to pull other security. Please, stay here."

Their gazes locked. Each man took the measure of the other.

Prescott grinned. "I worked with your brother."

"I know."

"Carry on, Mr. Steele."

While Prescott returned to his seat, Mason signaled his man who had earlier locked the terrace door and instructed him to accompany them, bringing up the rear. When the children and Lexie had gathered, Mason opened the door onto the flagstone terrace and stepped outside into a rose-colored dusk.

He led the way down a wide set of stone stairs to a wooden door. Like the rest of the hotel, this entrance was less than a decade old, but had been aged to look antique. What did they call it? Distressed. The wood had been distressed to make it seem as though this door and the stone wall were part of a hundred-year-old hunting lodge. In contrast, the door was opened by a computer pad that required Mason to enter a code. He opened the door and led them into the parking lot under the hotel.

The sound of their footsteps made a hollow echo in the concrete structure filled with vehicles. Many of the guests at the banquet were also staying at the hotel. Tomorrow, some of them would play golf with Admiral Prescott, which was another complicated scenario for TST Security.

Mason had already checked out the parking garage. With four separate exits on each level and six elevators, it was a good place to bring the kids for an escape. He hustled his little crew toward the elevators.

The teenagers were mature enough to know that something wasn't exactly copacetic. The oldest girl held the youngest boy's hand. These were military kids; they knew how to behave. Not so much for the Hollywood twins—handsome ten-year-olds with shaggy blond hair and dark eyebrows. They were punching each other, whining about how they wanted pizza and making growling noises interspersed with high-pitched squeaks.

Lexie hustled the gruesome twosome forward. Throughout this whole process she'd kept her cool and followed instructions. Mason noticed that she was carrying the emergency alert equipment Carlos had given her. If she ran into a threat, she was supposed to hit the red button and all TST Security personnel would respond.

He wondered if she'd had any specialized training to protect the kids. She was in good shape, had an athletic stride and her arms were well toned. But did Franny the nanny do kung fu?

He wanted to know more about her. Maybe tonight after the kids were in bed, they could get together. Maybe they'd talk, maybe laugh, maybe she'd allow him to glide his fingers down her smooth, tanned shoulders and arms. At the elevators, she shot him an over-the-shoulder glance before turning her full attention to the twins, who were trying to expand their obnoxious behavior to include the other kids. She moved quickly to separate the twins from the rest of the herd.

But one of the twins shoved into the teenage boy, Eddy Jr., who was at the age when he was almost manly. In a voice that was significantly deeper than that of

the twins, he muttered, "Watch what you're doing, dork face."

"You're not the boss of me."

"But he's bigger than you." His twin poked him in the back. "He could kick your—"

"Enough," Lexie said.

She stepped between the twins and Eddy Jr. Both elevators dinged as the doors opened simultaneously. Lexie entered one elevator and dragged the twins with her. "The three of us will take this one. We'll meet the rest of you on the seventh floor."

"Wait!" Mason said. This wasn't procedure. The kids should be accompanied by a bodyguard at all times.

She flashed him a wide grin. "Don't worry. I've got this."

The elevator door snapped closed, and he was left with a vision of her dark eyes sparkling. Her expression was full of mischief and something more. There was something mysterious about her, and he wondered what she knew that he didn't. She seemed to be laughing inside as though she had the punch line to an untold joke.

Chapter Two

In the elevator, Lexie stood between the twins and glared at the wood-paneled walls. The boutique hotel's impersonation of an old-time hunting lodge was beginning to annoy her. She didn't mind the elk and moose heads mounted on the walls in the lobby. After all, her dad and three older brothers had taken her on her first hunting trip when she was eight years old, and she understood their desire for occasional taxidermy.

But a real hunter would never stay at a place like this. Not with the golf course, the fake Persian rugs, the ornate imitation antique furniture and the kitschy Old West touches, like brass spittoons. Spittoons? This pricey hotel didn't allow smoking, much less chewing tobacco.

"You ticked off that bodyguard," said the twin named Caine.

"He'll get over it."

The other twin—who she always thought should have been named Abel but was actually Shane—tilted his head to one side and gave her a freakishly mature look. "I think you like that bodyguard."

How could he possibly know that? The kid was right, of course. She was drawn to Mason like a spinster moth to a muscular flame, but she didn't intend to discuss her personal feelings with the kids. "Mr. Steele seems like a nice man."

Caine tugged her right arm. "You really like him."

Shane snickered. "You want to marry him."

Ignoring the twins, she stared at the lighted numbers for the floors as they passed the fourth. An interruption would be most welcome, but she wasn't having any such luck. The twin monsters prattled back and forth about how she wanted to kiss Mason and "do it" with him, about how she was in love with him.

Though tempted to respond with a childish and extra loud "am not," she kept her voice trained to a calm level. "That's enough."

"But we got more, lots more."

"If I hear another word from either of you, there will be no pizza tonight, no ice cream, no TV, no computer games, no nothing. We clear?"

They went silent, nodded and stood up straight. Though the boys were only ten, they'd had a growth spurt and were almost as tall as she was at five feet three inches. Like golden retriever puppies, their feet and hands were too large for their gangly bodies. Someday they'd be huge, handsome dudes like their matinee idol father.

She liked big men, but not big babies like the twins' irresponsible daddy. She preferred a guy like Mason who was physically fit and in the business of protecting other people. A steady, stable guy, someone she could count on, a man she could trust.

Rein it in, Lexie. Sure, Mason was handsome with his buzz haircut and his square jaw and his butane-blue eyes. But she knew nothing about his character. He might be a cheat or a liar. Being drawn to him wouldn't be the first time she'd been fooled by a man with a pretty face and muscular shoulders.

With a scowl, she reminded herself that she had no proof that Anton Karpov had betrayed her. He'd disappeared while doing a job that might be connected with the admiral. That was what he'd told her. Most likely, he'd been lying. The admiral had never heard of Anton and didn't recognize him from photos.

At the seventh floor, the elevator dinged and the doors swept open. A man in a security guard uniform assigned by the hotel stood waiting, but she didn't recognize him. He didn't look like an employee, not with that stubble on his face.

She sensed a threat. She could smell it. Spreading her arms, she kept the twins on the elevator. Down the hall on the left, she glimpsed a body on the floor.

Backing into the elevator again, she said to the phony security man, "Oops, I forgot something."

When she reached back and hit the elevator button for the lobby, he reacted. His arm blocked the door from closing. He grabbed her shoulder. "You ain't going nowhere."

Lexie hit the red alert button for TST Security and said to the twins, "Go to the lobby."

She shoved the guard in the chest, keeping him away

from the twins. Lexie went on the offensive. Her first flying kick was aimed at the guard's midsection. He bent double. She fired another kick at his right kneecap.

Behind her back, she heard the elevator doors snap shut. The twins were safe. Good, she'd do anything to keep these kids from harm.

The fake guard clutched at his gut. His knee bent sideways as he made a gurgling noise in the back of his throat. Then he collapsed onto the fancy Persian carpet and rolled around while grabbing his injured leg.

She had to move fast. Where there was one thug, there would be others, and she didn't want to take on the whole gang with no other weapon than her karate skills. Lexie delivered another sharp kick to the head of the first thug. He went limp, unconscious. Since she'd chosen flats instead of pointy-toe stiletto heels for tonight's event, this fake guard might survive.

She dropped to her knees beside him and yanked his gun from the holster. Aiming high, she fired at two other men who were running toward her.

Her warning shots had the desired effect. The phony hotel guards sought cover, which gave her a few seconds to locate a better position.

MIDWAY THROUGH HIS elevator ascent with the children, Mason heard the warning squawk from Lexie's emergency alert button. What the hell? Had she run into trouble on the seventh floor? The sound of gunfire overhead was his answer.

He jabbed the elevator button, stopping the car on the sixth instead of the seventh floor. When the doors opened, he spoke to the other bodyguard. "Take the children to the lobby."

"What about you?"

"I'm going up."

Leaving the elevator, he listened to the babble of confused voices coming through his headset. They had all gotten the alert from Lexie. He heard Sean take control inside the banquet hall. Following procedure, Sean ordered most of the other TST guards to the front lobby, where Dylan—who was stationed at the reservation desk—would organize their operation.

The gunfire from above had not abated. What the hell was going on up there? He gave Sean an update. "It's Mason. I'm going up to the seventh floor where shots are being fired."

"Copy that," Dylan responded from the lobby. "I have the twins and the other kids. All secure."

The children were safe. Good. "What about Lexie, the nanny?"

"The twins say she's on the seventh floor."

Mason's gut clenched. If anything had happened to her because he'd let her take the elevator alone, he would never forgive himself. He spoke into the headset. "I'll be out of touch for a few minutes."

He unscrewed the earbud and welcomed the attending silence. His entire focus needed to be on Lexie.

Drawing his gun from the shoulder holster, he sprinted down the hotel corridor and through the door below the red Exit sign. He rushed up the concrete staircase to the seventh floor and eased his way through, moving carefully until he got his bearings.

The difference in decor on each floor was as subtle as the varying shades of beige on the wallpaper above the waist-high wood wainscoting. Antique-looking picture frames held sepia photos from the early 1900s, including many of Theodore Roosevelt, who was known for hunting in the Colorado Rockies and for establishing the National Park Service. Against the wall opposite the elevators was a claw-foot table with a floral arrangement and a teddy bear with the stuffing blown out of its chest. An unconscious man in a hotel uniform lay on the floor. Good guy or bad?

There was no sure way of telling. Down the hall was another unconscious man wearing only his underwear. Quick conclusion: the men who had been stripped were the real guards. The uniforms were being worn by impostors.

The *rat-a-tat* of automatic gunfire came from his left.

There were only fourteen rooms on this deluxe level, including a massive suite for the admiral and his wife. The floor plan was a B-shape with the elevators in the middle. Peering around the corner, he spotted the backsides of two uniformed men. When they tried to advance, a single shot repelled them. Lexie? Where did she get the gun?

Mason fired twice and got two hits. Both men reacted but neither went down. They must be wearing Kevlar vests under their uniform shirts. When they turned toward him, he saw Lexie dash across the end of the hallway. He hoped she'd run to the relative safety of her room.

No such luck.

While he and the impostor guards exchanged fire, she circled all the way around and came up behind him. "Mason, do you have another gun?"

"Not for you."

"Don't be a jerk. I've only got one bullet left."

"Where's your room?" he asked.

She pointed behind them and waved her key card. "It's over here. I'm not sure it's safe. There are two other thugs who aren't wearing uniforms. They could be hiding inside."

They were outnumbered, and the bad guys had more firepower. The best option was to retreat. "Take me to your room, unlock the door and I'll enter first to make sure it's safe. Then you follow me in."

"You and me in the bedroom? Well, that's the best offer I've had in a long time."

He didn't take his eyes off the two men who were laying down a steady barrage of gunfire; he didn't need to look at her to know she was grinning. Calm under pressure, he liked that. What he didn't like was the way she squatted down and tugged at his pant leg. "What are you doing?"

"Looking for your ankle holster. Aha!" She undid the snap and took his second weapon. "Thanks, I need this."

She hustled down the hallway, and he followed. At her room, she unlocked the door and stepped aside. He entered, holding his gun with both hands as he searched the bathroom, the closet and under the beds. "All clear."

Instead of obeying his instructions to follow him inside and lock the door, she braced herself in the doorway and dropped to one knee as she fired down the hallway. It was obvious that she knew what she was doing. Earlier, he'd been wondering if she had self-defense instruction. The answer to that question was a resounding yes. Lexie was dangerous.

When he pulled her inside and closed the door, he noticed the slash of red across her upper arm. "You're bleeding."

"Just a graze, but it really stings." She looked down at the angled cut that dripped blood down to her elbow. "That's going to leave a scar."

He dragged a heavy silk-upholstered chair and positioned it in front of the doorway. He added a desk. The barricade would slow down any attacker long enough for him to get off a couple of accurate shots.

From the bathroom, he grabbed a fluffy white hand towel and brought it to where she was sitting on a carved wooden bench in front of a mirrored dressing table. He wrapped the towel around her wounded arm and brushed escaped curls off her forehead. Under her freckles, her complexion had faded to a waxy pale.

"Are you all right?" he asked.

"Sure. Fine."

When the energizing effect of adrenaline wore off, he expected her to crash like a rock slide. And he wanted to be there when she unwound, to catch her before she fell, to hold her and tell her that life was going to get better. There was something about her that awakened his protective instincts.

As a rule, he kept his distance from other people and avoided committed relationships. Losing his brother had torn a hole in his heart and made him wary of deep connections. But Lexie's grin repaired his pain. He wanted to be close to her.

He held her hand, marveling at her slender fingers and the delicate turn of her wrist. His gaze lifted to her dark eyes. "I won't let anything bad happen to you."

"I know you'll do your best." She shrugged. "Sometimes there's no way to prevent the bad stuff."

Though she was acting nonchalant, the hollow echo in her voice surprised him. He could tell that this woman had experienced more than her fair share of tragedy. Immediately curious, he wanted to hear more about her life, her dreams and her plans for the future.

But this wasn't the right time. Gently, he removed his gun from her clenched fingers. Her vulnerability touched him, but he also appreciated her strength. When she'd needed to be tough, she held off four bad guys—five including the unconscious one outside the elevator. Now she could relax.

He didn't have that respite. An aggressive burst of gunfire echoed in the corridor like a call to duty. He stuck his earbud back in. Sean was screaming his name, demanding an update and informing Mason that they had a group ready to storm the seventh floor.

Gun in hand, he turned his attention to TST Security business.

Chapter Three

Leaving Mason to growl orders on his intercom, Lexie slipped into the bathroom, locked the door and leaned against it. Stillness wrapped around her. Inside this pristine tile and marble cubicle, the gunfire seemed far away.

Exhaling a sigh, she slid down the wall. *Sanctuary!* Not that she was truly safe. This peaceful feeling was akin to being in the eye of a tornado while danger continued to swirl, but she was glad for the momentary respite—especially glad she'd made it into the bathroom before she swooned like some kind of whimpering Southern belle.

Mason didn't need to know she was scared. She liked him and wanted him to like her. And something told her that he wasn't the kind of guy who enjoyed being around girlie girls. She'd seen the gleam in his eye when he watched her taking aim and when he tended to her bullet wound. As if on cue, the red-stained towel fell from her arm. Oozing blood smeared and saturated the blue fabric of her jumpsuit.

"Bummer." This was one of her favorite outfits.

It didn't hurt. Not much, anyway. But her body was having a reaction that was out of proportion to the injury. Was this some kind of panic attack? She was acutely tense. Her muscles twisted into knots. Her gut clenched. Other symptoms slammed into her, one after the other. She was light-headed. Her breathing was labored, and she smelled the odor of rotting meat. The inside of her mouth tasted like ash. Shivers twitched across her shoulders.

Her spine buckled, and she ratcheted down to the floor. She lay on her side with her wounded arm up, the white marble cooling her cheek. She tried to breathe deeply and calm herself. But she was too tense...and too cold, ice-cold. Her fists clenched between her breasts. Her pulse pounded. She pinched her eyes closed, hoping to blot out the terrible fear that threatened to overwhelm her.

She had to get control. *I'm going to be all right.* No matter how many times her conscious mind repeated those words, a deeper place in her soul didn't believe it. *I won't die.* Post-traumatic stress squeezed her in a grip so tight that her bones rattled. *Everything is going to be all right.* She wasn't in mortal danger, not this time. *This isn't like the accident.*

Her memory jolted. Flung backward in time, she heard a fierce metallic crunch and the explosion of the air bag from the steering wheel. Her brother's little bronze sedan had been thrown onto its side and was skidding toward the edge of the cliff near Buena Vista. Cringing, she heard the grinding screech of her car door against the pavement. *Should have taken the truck.* Jake was going to kill her for wrecking his car. *Not my fault.* The other car—black with tinted windows—had crossed the center line and hit her front fender.

Her mouth opened wide as she desperately tried to scream. The air bag had stolen her breath. She could only gasp. And then her brother's car was falling, crashing end over end, down the steep hillside and into the trees.

Other people had told her that they couldn't recall a single moment of their accidents. In the midst of their traumatic events, they experienced amnesia. Not her. She felt every twist and turn as the car plummeted. Fully conscious, she braced herself for what would surely come next: the gas explosion that would tear her limbs apart and the flames that would sear her flesh.

That wasn't the way it turned out. Though the driver who had hit her fled the scene, there was a witness in another vehicle. She was rescued, taken to the hospital and stitched back together. The doctors fixed as much as they could.

Replaying the accident—the worst moments of her life—lessened her current panic. The terror that had threatened to smother her receded into the shadows of her mind. She forced her thoughts back to the present reality and focused on what had just happened. She'd been attacked by five armed men.

Instead of sliding deeper into fear, she chuckled to herself. This definitely wasn't like the horrible feeling of helplessness in the car accident. When it came to self-defense, she did okay. Not a big surprise, as she'd been trained by her three older brothers, who ran a karate dojo. And her dad, a Marine Corps sergeant, had insisted that she know how to handle rifles, pistols, handguns and other weaponry.

Thinking of the DeMille men calmed her. Even though they were a thousand miles away in Austin, Texas, they were watching over her. They'd made her into what she was today: an independent, stubborn, kick-ass tomboy. A survivor.

When she'd encountered the first man outside the elevator, she knew—without the slightest doubt—that she could take him down. Lexie had earned her brown belt in karate when she was fifteen.

Shooting at people was more difficult; she didn't want to kill anybody. If Mason hadn't shown up, she had no idea what she would have done. He'd taken a risk by charging onto this floor to help her. Of course, security was his job...but still, she was grateful.

There was a tap on the door. "Lexie, are you all right?"

She scrambled to get her legs under her. "I'm fine."

"Are you sure? It's quiet in there."

"I'm fine," she repeated.

She should have turned on the shower. Mason wouldn't have knocked if he'd heard water running. Struggling, she lunged to her feet and hit the faucet in the sink. There! Was that enough proof enough that she was fine and dandy?

Her reflection in the mirror confronted her. Not a pretty sight! Her arm dripped blood, her makeup was smudged and her ponytail was tangled like a bird's nest. What she needed was a shower, but stripping off her clothes while bad guys were on the prowl seemed like an invitation to more trouble—naked trouble.

She went to the bathroom door, pressed her ear against it and listened for the sounds of battle from the outer corridor. There were distant pops. This wasn't the kind of cheesy motel where you heard every cough and sputter from the neighboring room, but gunfire was loud. She expected to hear somethi—

"Lexie?" Mason knocked again.

She jumped backward with a yelp. Off balance, she stumbled into the wall beside the huge Plexiglas shower with four separate spray nozzles. "Fine," she shouted. "I'm perfectly fine."

He opened the door.

"I locked that," she said.

"And I picked the lock." He strode toward her.

Whether she wanted his protection or not, Mason was here. He guided her across the marble floor and lifted her onto the counter with double sinks. "Do you want the outfit on or off?"

"On, of course." She pushed at his chest, accidentally staining his light blue shirt with blood. "Jeez Louise, I'm sorry."

"Jeez Louise?" He lifted an eyebrow.

"I don't swear. It's a nanny thing."

"Did you used to?"

"Hell, yes." She felt a grin spread across her face, and she was amazed by how swiftly her mood had transformed. Mason was magic. "I have three brothers."

He nodded. "Every other word was obscene."

"Not as much as you'd think. Dad didn't tolerate bad language."

"Was he a religious man?"

"Worse. A marine sergeant. Discipline was his middle name."

"My older brother was in the corps. He worked with the admiral in the Middle East." His shoulders flexed in a tense shrug. "I'd like to think that one of the reasons TST Security was hired was the admiral's good opinion of my brother."

Being from a military family, she was sensitive to the fact that he spoke of his brother in the past tense. "I wonder if your brother knew my dad, Daniel DeMille? He was stationed in the Middle East, too. He retired five years ago."

"My brother was killed six years ago in Afghanistan."

"I'm sorry."

"So am I." He peeled off his suit jacket, tossed it into the bedroom and started rolling up his shirtsleeves. "Now I'm going to clean your wound."

She pointed toward the open bathroom door. "What about those thugs in the hallway?"

"My partners have it under control. The local police and sheriff are on the way." He tapped the listening device in his ear. "TST Security has rounded up all but one of the bad guys. He locked himself in a room down the hall and thinks he's safe."

His full lips quirked in a wry smile that told her the criminal hiding in one of the rooms was making a big mistake. She asked, "What's going to happen to him?"

"While he's watching the door to the hallway, one of the snipers on the roof is going to bust through a window."

"And you'd like to watch," she said.

"Oh, yeah."

His tone reminded her of the DeMille men, but there was nothing brotherly about the tingling she felt when he touched her arm. He moistened a washcloth under the hot water she'd been running in the sink. Holding her arm below the elbow, he cautiously wiped away the blood.

"The cut isn't too deep," he said. "I don't think you'll need stitches, but you should have a doc take a look."

"Sure." While he focused on taking care of her, she studied him. Her father would approve of his buzz cut and no-nonsense attitude, but she was more impressed by his deep-set dark blue eyes and high cheekbones. His tanned forearms showed that he spent time outdoors, but her thoughts about him required an indoor setting... A bedroom scenario, to be specific.

He lifted his gaze. What would it be like to wake up and see those eyes looking back at her? He was almost too handsome, too good to be true. *Please, Mason, don't be a liar or a cheat.*

Using a clean towel, he patted her arm dry. When he reached behind her head, unfastened her ponytail and let her curly hair fall to her shoulders, his face was near hers. If she tilted her head and leaned in, their lips would touch.

Impulsively, her fingers snatched his striped silk necktie, and she held him in place. He was mere inches away from her, so very close that she felt the heat radiating from his body. She smelled his aftershave, a citrus and nutmeg flavor with a hint of something else… the indefinable scent of a man.

"You smell good." She hadn't intended her voice to become a purr, but that was what happened.

"So do you."

Her gaze twined with his, and she tugged at his necktie to pull him a half inch closer. She wanted to kiss him, but the situation was messy. She was sitting on the countertop at a weird angle. If she pressed her body against his chest, she'd smear the blood all over his shirt. More important, she barely knew this man and could be setting herself up for a world of embarrassment.

He ended her indecision. She should have known that he would. Mason was a take-charge kind of guy. He buried his fingers in her untamed hair and held the back of her skull so that he was supporting her. Then he kissed her.

Crazy, wild sensations bloomed inside her. He kissed the same way he seemed to do everything else: with skill and finesse. His lips were firm, and he exerted exactly the right amount of pressure.

His tongue traced the line of her mouth, slipped inside and probed against her teeth. She opened wider for him. Her tongue joined with his and—

There was a hammering noise from the door to the hallway. A deep voice shouted, "Mason, you in there?"

They broke apart so quickly that she bit the inside of her cheek. "Bad timing," she muttered.

"I have to go."

Twenty questions popped inside her head. *Can I see you again? Will there be another kiss? Can I give you my phone number?* She said only one word aloud. "Thanks."

"For what?"

"Saving my life."

He dropped a light kiss on her forehead. "My pleasure."

As she watched him walk out the door, she whispered, "The pleasure was all mine."

PEERING THROUGH THE infrared scope of his rifle, Anton Karpov scanned the windows on the seventh floor of the mountain hotel, trying to catch a glimpse of Franny. Earlier tonight, he had watched her through the crosshairs on his scope. She'd been outside on the terrace, meeting and greeting, laughing and smiling. She looked good—damn good. Until tonight, he hadn't paid any attention to the nanny.

But now he knew. Anton had positively identified Franny DeMille, the chick he'd almost moved in with. Why was she calling herself Lexie? How the hell did she get to be a nanny?

The Franny he knew was a kick-ass daredevil who couldn't care less about kids and didn't know a damn thing about taking care of them. When he was dating her, she'd told him—flat out—that she didn't want babies. Hey, great news for him. He wasn't meant to play daddy. He wasn't serious about her, either. Still, it made him mad when she dumped him. It was supposed to be the other way around. He made sure she knew that.

His cell phone vibrated in his pocket, and he answered.

The voice on the other end was the leader himself. There had been a lot of talk at meetings about how no single person was more important than another. They were equals. Some had special skills or areas of expertise, but their group didn't operate within the structure of a hierarchy.

Anton didn't buy in to any of that phony, mealy-mouthed philosophy. While others talked about all for one and "the greater good," he held his silence. There was only one truth he believed in: dollars and cents. He'd been associated with the leader for almost ten years, performing special tasks for decent pay.

Quietly, the leader said, "Move out. I'll contact you later, Tony."

Long ago, Anton had Americanized his name to Tony Curtis after the old-time movie star. He even looked kind of like that Tony, with his curly black hair and blue eyes. The real Tony Curtis was usually cast as a pretty boy hero, and that didn't suit Anton Karpov, not at all. He only changed his mind when he saw the movie star play the role of Albert DeSalvo, widely believed to be the Boston Strangler.

"Are you sure I should go, sir?" He was one of the few who knew the leader's real name, but he seldom spoke it. "I have a couple of angles for a clear shot."

"I'm tempted, Tony. I'd like to kill those idiots who got caught."

"Is there any chance they won't spill their guts?"

"Oh, they'll talk. The admiral's men are skilled interrogators."

"Is that a problem?"

"They don't know enough to worry about. They're unimportant."

The leader didn't seem concerned about losing five men. The less influential members of Anti-Conspiracy Committee for Democracy, also known as AC-CD, had access to a limited amount of information. They were assigned simple jobs. Tonight, the only thing they'd been required to do was disable the hotel security and fill in for them, leaving the way open for more experienced operatives. The trained, experienced staff, led by Anton/Tony, would have kidnapped the admiral.

Anton/Tony slung his rifle over his shoulder and rose to his feet. "It was the nanny who messed up the plan."

"How could a little girl like that be such a big problem?"

The leader didn't know her. For a couple of seconds, Tony felt superior to the man who usually gave the orders. For a change, it was Tony who had the ace up his sleeve, information the leader wasn't privy to, and he was tempted to hold back.

But he didn't care about showing how smart he was and gaining power in AC-CD. He was after a quick payday, and the best way to separate the leader from his cash was to show him something he might want to buy. Franny was a prize he could set before the leader.

"She says her name is Lexie, but I recognized her

tonight. The nanny is a karate expert. It's Franny De-Mille, my old girlfriend."

"You don't say." The leader's voice dropped to a low, thoughtful level. "If you asked her to help you, would she?"

"We didn't break up on good terms, but I could always get her to do what I wanted." Not exactly true, but he wished it so. When he'd been with her, he was a better man. "She'll do what I say."

"I'll be in touch."

Before leaving his sniper nest, Tony pulled up his balaclava to cover the lower part of his face. Silently and stealthily, he made his way through the forest. His experience as a hunting guide was why he'd been pegged for this assignment. He could be trusted to blend with nature and not be seen. And his skill at marksmanship was worthy of a world-class assassin.

Chapter Four

In the rustic-style foyer outside the banquet hall, Mason conferred quietly with his partner Dylan, whose tall, wiry frame had been transformed from nerdy to sophisticated by a tailored black suit and a striped silk tie. Likewise, his messy brown hair had been tamed in a ponytail at the nape of his neck. They were waiting for the admiral's wife to leave the hall and join them. Prescott had asked them to escort her to the conference room, where he and several branches of law enforcement and the military had gathered.

"NSA, CIA, Interpol, army and navy intelligence," Dylan said. He pushed his horn-rimmed glasses up on his nose. "The gang's all here."

"How do you know their affiliations?"

"They were all at the banquet." As part of security procedure, he had vetted the invited guests and used facial recognition software to make sure they matched their stated identity. "Some of these guys are high-ranking hotshots. On six of them, I got an 'access denied' message when I searched for further info."

"Did you?" Mason asked. "Tell me the truth. Did you dig deeper?"

"Not yet."

But he could if the need arose. Dylan was a skilled hacker, capable of breaching NSA or CIA security without leaving a trace. He'd already patched Admiral Prescott through to the offices of the Secretary of the Navy on a video server so that SecNav could join the meeting in the conference room.

The sound of laughter erupted from inside the banquet hall. For the past hour, the guests had been watching a PowerPoint presentation that outlined the medical and sanitation needs of children in sub-Saharan Africa.

Mason glanced over at his partner. "We did good."

"How do you figure?"

"All five bad guys have been taken into custody."

"Have they?" Dylan arched an eyebrow in a skeptical expression that irritated Mason to no end. "The so-called baddies are still in the hotel."

The local sheriff, Colorado law enforcement and NSA were all fighting over who would take possession of these low-level thugs. "Arresting them isn't our problem."

"What if there are others?"

"We'll handle it. This assignment still counts as a success for TST Security." And for him, personally. Not only had he shown Admiral Prescott, a man he admired, that he was competent, but he'd also met Lexie. Her grin lifted his spirits. Their kiss elevated the evening into noteworthy; he'd remember that short, sweet contact for a very long time.

Dylan slouched and jammed his fists into his pockets, distorting the crisp line of his suit. "I don't like this, Mace. Too many questions. Not enough answers. We don't know why those guys invaded the seventh floor or what they were after."

"Whatever it was, they didn't get it. We stopped them. We met our objectives." Mason ticked off their achievements on his fingers. "The admiral and his family are safe. None of the good guys, not even the hotel guards, were seriously injured. And the people who came here for a banquet are still having their coffee and chocolate mousse dessert."

"I'd approximate that eighty-five percent of the guests are oblivious of the attack."

Though he had no idea where Dylan got his percentage, Mason assumed that his computer-geek partner was correct. Most of the guests had remained in their chairs while the servers cleared away their plates and refilled their wineglasses. Some of them might have looked around when they heard the sound of approaching police sirens, but the flashing red-and-blue lights weren't visible from the banquet hall, and the hotel management people were doing everything in their power to make sure their guests weren't aware of the mayhem on the seventh floor.

The door swept open and Helena Christie Prescott charged toward them. She was a classic beauty with long raven hair and a killer body, but all Mason saw were her flared nostrils and the flames shooting from her green eyes as she demanded, "What the hell is going on?"

"Your husband asked that I bring you—"

"Edgar is all right, isn't he?"

"Yes, ma'am."

"That's good, because I'm going to hurt him, hurt him bad." She had morphed from fiery dragon into sinister assassin, a role she'd played in a movie Mason saw. The assassin might even have used that line about hurting him bad. "And the children?"

"Everybody's okay." Mason gestured toward the hallway. "Come with us to the conference room, where your husband can brief you."

"Lead on." She strode along beside him, leaving Dylan in their wake. In her five-inch heels, she almost matched Mason's six-foot-three-inch height, and she hiked up the side of her gown opposite the slit so she could move faster.

Dylan—the coward—had cleverly fallen back, leaving Mason to deal with Helena. He was certain that any comment from him about not worrying or calming down would not be prudent.

"We're almost there," he said. "It's on this floor."

She came to a sudden halt. "I'm not being the least bit unreasonable. But what am I to think? My husband gets called away by his assistant, then the military guys and four agents—two CIA and two from some weird NSA department—slide out the door. What the hell is happening? Has Aspen been invaded by terrorists?"

Mason couldn't have been happier to see Lexie step out of the elevator and come toward them. A short while ago, he'd saved the nanny's life. Now it was her turn to save him.

She'd changed into casual clothes: sneakers, jeans and a long forest-green sweatshirt. Her wild auburn hair was held back from her face by a yellow band.

Helena spotted her and flung both arms around Lexie in a dramatic hug. "Thank God you're here."

Though jolted back on her heels, Lexie recovered her balance and spoke calmly. "Everything is going to be fine."

"Is it? Is it really?"

"Sure," Lexie said. "The kids are okay. They're all together in your suite. I left the hotel babysitter to keep an eye on them. Plus two of the TST bodyguards." She glanced at Mason and mouthed, *Is Carlos all right?*

He gave her a thumbs-up. The big guy had recovered and was sheepish about being sick. Since there didn't seem to be a connection between his stomach flu and the ambush on the seventh floor, he doubted that poison was involved. Carlos was once again in charge of guarding the children.

"Why wouldn't the kids be fine?" Helena asked. "Has there been a threat?"

Lexie turned to him. "You haven't told her?"

"The admiral wanted to explain himself."

A ringtone—a song from *Mary Poppins*—sounded, and Lexie retrieved her cell phone from a sweatshirt pocket. After a glance at the caller ID, she looked back at the admiral's wife. Her eyes narrowed. "Your husband has some serious explaining to do. Where is he?"

Mason opened the door to the conference room and stepped out of the way as the two women marched inside. Most of the people seated around the long table were men. One of the two women wore US Marine Corps dress blues, while the other was super chic, probably a higher-up in the CIA who shopped in Paris. In keeping with the early-1900s hunting lodge theme, the conference room was wood-paneled with elk, deer and bear heads on the walls. The snarling grizzly over the stone fireplace matched Helena's fierce expression.

Prescott leaped to his feet. "I believe you all know my wife, Helena Christie Prescott. And this is our nanny, Lexie DeMille."

The chic older woman applauded Lexie. "Impressive job, young lady. If you're ever looking for a job, contact me."

"She's not looking," Helena said curtly. "Edgar Prescott, step outside with me, please."

Without saying a word, Mason sent the admiral a mental warning. *Do what she says, man. Your wife is ticked off enough to play an assassin in real life. And you're her target.*

Apparently, Prescott's antennae were working well enough to pick up on the message. He excused himself, stepped away from the table and went into the hallway. As soon as the door to the conference room closed, he apologized to his wife.

Though this was a private conversation, Mason and his partner had to be there. It was their job to guard these two bodies. They were far less uncomfortable than Lexie who shuffled her feet and stared into the distance, pretending to be somewhere else.

"I didn't want to upset you," the admiral said to his wife. "There were gunshots fired on the seventh floor."

"Our floor?"

"Lexie was involved," he continued, "and, as you can plainly see, she's fine. TST Security rounded up the bad guys and took care of the threat. We're safe. There's nothing to worry about."

Not quite true. Mason found the situation worrisome, but that might just be his naturally vigilant nature. Overall, he was satisfied that they were safe. Choppers were airborne and searching. Local law enforcement had set up a perimeter around the hotel and would be escorting those who were leaving to their cars. There were enough armed officers patrolling in the hotel that Mason and TST Security were almost redundant.

"Very well," Helena said as she linked her arm with her husband's. "Come back to the banquet hall with me and give your speech."

"I should stay here." He looked over his shoulder at the closed door to the conference room, and then he turned to his wife. "Is there any way I can convince you to give my speech for me?"

"My dah-ling, don't be absurd. These people want to hear from you. I've only visited Africa a few times. You lived there. You know what this charity is all about."

He lifted her hand to his lips and kissed her manicured fingertips. "On our last trip to Madagascar, I remember how you took over the school and taught the kids how to sing."

Mason made eye contact with Dylan, who was being so unobtrusive that he was nearly invisible. He and his partner, both of them single, could take lessons from the admiral as he wove a charmed web around his formerly furious wife.

Helena rubbed against his arm like a slinky panther wanting to be stroked. "I had fun with my little friends, my little *marafiki*. And I loved the midnight spice market in Madagascar. But the people at this banquet have contributed a great deal of money, and they deserve the full package."

"I'm playing golf with the big investors tomorrow."

"Everybody else expects to hear a talk from you."

"Fine." He kissed her hand again. "I'll come in with you and give a brief hello. Then I'm heading back to the conference room and you can talk."

"About what?"

"I think you know," he said. "These people are educated, philanthropic, intelligent and discerning. They'll want to know about Hollywood."

"They always do," she said as she adjusted his necktie and patted his bottom.

Before they went into the banquet room, the admiral turned toward him and said, "Mason, wait for me out here."

Applause sounded as the door closed behind them. Dylan dodged around him, grabbed Lexie's hand and gave a firm shake. "From what I hear, you kicked butt. Martial arts?"

"My brothers run a karate dojo in Austin. I was starting to teach a couple of classes of my own before I became a nanny."

Mason liked the way her eyes crinkled at the corners and her mouth turned up at the edges. He didn't so much like to see her grinning at his partner. "Dylan, I thought you were anxious to return to the front desk."

"I am?"

Mason wanted her all to himself, even though they only had a few moments and limited privacy. He tapped Dylan's arm a little bit harder than necessary to drive home the point. "Don't you need to be somewhere else?"

"Actually, I do." When he nodded, his glasses slid to the tip of his nose. "I have an audio and video recorder set on the conference room and it needs monitoring. So, I should go." Suiting the action to the words, he started walking backward while waving goodbye and mumbling about how busy he was.

Lexie turned that pretty smile on Mason, which was where it belonged. "Your partner is kind of a goofball."

"That's what happens with these genius types. They trip over their shoelaces because their brains are occupied with complicated problems."

Her gaze flicked toward the doors to the banquet room and then focused on him. "I need to talk to Prescott. Do you think I'll get a chance? I just need a few minutes."

"It shouldn't be a problem." He gently took her left arm—the one that wasn't injured—and escorted her across the open space outside the banquet hall to an antique-looking red leather love seat. "How's the bullet wound?"

"Just a graze," she said. "I'm fine. The hotel doctor patched me up and slapped on a bandage."

She perched nervously on the edge of the small sofa. On duty, Mason seldom allowed himself to sit; he needed to be on his feet and ready to move at the first sign of a threat. But the man he was guarding was inside another room where there were at least three other TST Security men. He sat beside Lexie, thigh to thigh. It would have been easy to rest his arm on the back of the love seat, but he exercised restraint.

"Prescott will talk to you," he assured her. "He's got to be grateful to you for keeping his kids safe."

"I hate to bother him with my problems. He put up with a lot of mistakes from me when I was learning the ropes. Being a nanny is more than babysitting, you know, especially when you're working with smart kids."

When she spoke, she gestured with her hands, but most of her animation came from her face. She punctuated her sentences with lifts of her eyebrows, scowls and grins and even a twitch of her freckled nose. The light makeup she'd worn at dinner had been wiped away, but she still looked good. He could watch her for hours and not get bored. "Did you get training on how to be a nanny? Did you go to nanny school?"

"I have a degree in psychology. Not that my studies help when Shane and Caine are punching each other. Or little Stella loses her magic wand." She grimaced and smirked at the same time. "I could probably use some instruction. I kind of lucked into this job, just showed up on Admiral Prescott's doorstep with no expectations. I didn't know they needed a nanny and didn't know I could be one."

"Tell me more."

"It was about a year ago. I was twenty-four, finished with college, living with my dad and working at the dojo. I didn't know what I wanted to do next. It needed to be something where I helped people, but I didn't know how or where. I liked the idea of working for something like the admiral's charity in sub-Saharan Africa." She tossed her head, setting her reddish curls into motion. "Or maybe not."

Somehow she'd gotten distracted. He pulled her back to the main topic. "Why were you on the admiral's doorstep?"

"There was this guy…" She paused and laughed. "How many wild stories have started off with those words? Anyway, this guy—his name was Anton—was kind of my boyfriend and he wanted to move in with me. Did I mention that I lived with my dad? Being the only girl in the family meant I did most of the cooking and shopping and laundry. In exchange, I didn't pay rent."

Once again, she'd gone skipping off on a tangent. He could feel her tension. Nervous energy had her running on high speed, making it hard to rein in her thoughts. He wanted to hold her and calm her down. Even though they had kissed, he had the feeling that this wasn't the right time. "When you were with your dad, did you like the arrangement?"

"I love my family. Living with Dad was comfortable. I'd work at the dojo, come home, cook dinner and handle a couple of chores. Then I'd do pretty much whatever I pleased. My biggest worry was that I'd get too cozy. On some fine day, I'd wake up and find out that I was seventy years old and never left home."

"Did you move in with Anton?"

"It was the other way around. He wanted to move

in with me, with my family, which was a little creepy. And I couldn't imagine asking my dad. No. Way."

"Glad to hear it."

"Don't get me wrong," she said. "My dad liked my boyfriend. The two of them bonded over their guns. Anton worked as a hunting guide and had some high-profile positions. He'd even worked for the admiral, which impressed my dad because he knew the Admiral Prescott, too. Anyway, I wanted to—"

"Wait."

He held up a palm, signaling her to stop. Lexie seemed to be bounding over the relevant portions of this story. She'd already mentioned that her father was stationed in the Middle East but never said he knew Prescott…and now her former boyfriend?

"Problem?" she asked.

"Your father, my brother and your boyfriend were all buddies with the admiral. That's an unbelievable coincidence."

"In the first place," she said, "I wouldn't exactly say they were buddies. More like acquaintances."

"You're right," he admitted.

"As for your brother and my dad, they were both in the Marine Corps, and both were stationed in the Middle East, where Admiral Prescott was one of the top guys running the show."

"What about the boyfriend?"

"He came looking for us because Prescott mentioned that he knew my dad and my dad lived in Austin. I met Anton through my father. I remember when I walked into the house and he saw me for the first time.

His jaw dropped…literally. He thought I was something special."

Though Mason had never met the guy and probably never would, he didn't like this Anton character. What kind of man tries to move in with the father of his girlfriend? "When he asked to move in with you, did he propose?"

"I wouldn't let him. He hinted and I shut him down. I wasn't looking to settle down and get married. I told him he couldn't move into my dad's house and he should think again about our relationship." She gave another one of her adorable shrugs. "He left me without saying goodbye. He left a note that told me to kiss off."

When she met his gaze, Mason saw anger and determination in her chocolate-brown eyes. Her expression was similar to when she was shooting at the fake security guys. Apparently, nobody told Lexie to kiss off and got away with it.

Now he understood how this twisted little story fit together. "You went looking for Anton."

"I wanted him to know that I broke up with him. Not the other way around. And I also wanted to get out of Austin for a while."

"You came to Colorado. To the admiral's doorstep."

"No sign of Anton. Prescott didn't remember him very well at all. Still, he invited me to stay for as long as I wanted, because of my dad." Her gaze drifted as she recalled. "I was surprised. I didn't think my dad was a big deal in the military, but I guess he was important enough for the admiral to think of him as a friend."

"And while you were there," Mason said, "you became the nanny."

"The nanny who was there when I arrived decided to quit. And I stepped in. I've never regretted it."

Her cell phone rang again.

She pulled it out and stared at the caller ID before she leaped to her feet. "Hi, Dad."

Chapter Five

Lexie's dad spoke in tough, uncompromising tones. Sure, he was retired, but he still hadn't stopped being the ultimate hard-ass Sergeant Major Daniel DeMille. "You listen to me, Franny, and you listen good."

"I'm not going by Franny anymore." She walked a few paces on the patterned hallway carpeting. "Call me Lexie."

"Your mother and I named you, and I'll call you whatever I damn well please, Miss Francine Alexandra DeMille."

The use of her full name was not a positive sign. Nor was the mention of her mother, who had divorced Daniel when Lexie was twelve. After Mom left, Dad didn't often link them together. In doing so, he seemed to be summoning up the ghost of a past that no longer existed. Perhaps it never had. Perhaps they had always been a dysfunctional family. With Mom gone, Grandma took over. And Dad was usually stationed on the other side of the world.

He growled. "You haven't returned my phone calls."

"I talked to you once and gave you my answer." She

paced farther down the hall, noting that Mason kept a discreet distance but stayed with her.

"That answer, your answer, is unsatisfactory."

"I'm not going to change my mind," she said. "I won't quit my job and run home because you're worried about me."

"Either you get your rear end back to Texas or I'm coming to get you."

"I'm putting you on hold."

"Why?"

Because I'm furious and don't want to say something I'll regret later. "Excuse me, Dad."

She clicked him to silence and shook her fist at the cell phone. Her lips pinched together in a tight knot. Then she exhaled in a whoosh, blowing through her pursed lips like air coming out of a balloon.

She whirled around and looked at Mason. "My dad is treating me like I'm five years old. He's ticked off about what happened on the seventh floor."

"Did Prescott call him?"

"It was his assistant, Josh Laurent. You've probably met him. Long, pointy nose. Beady eyes. Stooped shoulders. He looks like a woodpecker."

"Yeah." Mason wiped the smile off his face. "We've met."

"Good old Josh didn't do a very good job of telling my dad what happened." She stopped beside a tiny desk with carved legs and a brass spittoon to one side. "He made that stupid ambush sound terrible and dangerous."

"It was dangerous. Those were real bullets. The blood on your arm? That was real, too."

"Really real," she muttered under her breath.

"What?"

"There's real life, which is what life is supposed to be. And really real life, which is how it actually is. Okay, for example, I'm a nanny in real life. In really real, I'm also an assistant, a nurse, a secretary and a teacher."

"In these real and extra real worlds of yours, where do you put the bullets?"

"Whose side are you on?"

"Yours," he said without hesitation. "But if you were my daughter, I'd be worried about you."

Men! They were all alike, thinking that women were helpless creatures who couldn't survive without one of them standing at her side and flexing his biceps. She was an adult. Not daddy's baby girl. Lexie could take care of herself.

She hadn't always been so independent and strong. When she came home from the hospital after her accident, she'd had serious nerve damage. Some docs had predicted that she'd never walk again. Her internal injuries had resulted in life-altering surgeries. She was scared, so deeply scared that she'd prayed to go to sleep and never wake up. It had seemed that life was too much to handle.

That was when her father stepped up and faced the challenge. Whether she needed him or not, he was there. Day and night, he watched over her and nursed her back to health. His gentle manner kept her spirits up. His firm encouragement reinforced her progress in physical therapy, where she literally started with baby steps.

After four weeks of recovery, when she'd been able

to walk with crutches, she found out that he'd retired so he could take the time to be with her. Though he'd put in enough years with the military to qualify for a very nice pension and had plans for his retirement, she felt guilty about taking him away from a career he loved. The very last thing she wanted was to be a burden to her family.

She looked into Mason's steady blue eyes. "Why do you think my dad should worry about me?"

"Because he loves you."

Her tears sloshed and threatened to spill over her lower eyelids. Though the male of the species could be overbearing and pushy and demanding, they could also be achy-breaky sweet. All that blustering and flexing was the way they showed that they cared.

Once again, she was stabbed in the gut by guilt. She didn't want to upset her dad. "In your professional opinion, do you think it's dangerous for me to stay with the Prescott family?"

"I can only assess one situation at a time. Right now I'm pretty sure that everybody's safe. Do you want me to talk to your father?"

"Not a good idea. Right at the moment, he doesn't think much of your abilities, even though I mentioned that you saved my life. And I explained how I ignored your advice to ride up on the elevator by myself."

He pointed to the phone. "You can't keep him on hold forever."

"I'm going back to my original plan." She tapped on the cell phone screen. "Dad, I'm going to have you talk to Admiral Prescott. He can explain why it won't be dangerous."

"I'll be waiting for that call."

She rolled her eyes at the phone. "I know you will."

PRESCOTT EMERGED FROM the banquet hall in full sail, leaving cheers and applause in his wake. There wasn't time for Lexie to ask him to talk to her father or to do anything else. With long determined strides, the admiral charged down the hall toward the conference room with the animal heads on the walls.

Before entering, he paused and straightened his necktie. "Be ready to move, Mason. I intend to get out of here ASAP."

"I understand," Mason said.

"Do you?" Prescott lifted an eyebrow.

"I'm not a police officer, but I'm sure there hasn't been enough time for thorough questioning and investigation. Since you made the decision to stay at the hotel tonight, it seems wise to wait until morning, when you have enough information to know what needs to be done."

"My thoughts exactly."

Lexie felt like cheering. Mason's rational assessment made the crazy situation seem manageable. Not like her father, who was probably out by the barn shooting tin cans off the fence.

Mason said, "Lexie has something she needs to talk to you about."

"Of course." He pivoted to face her, held her at arm's

length and peered into her eyes. "How are you holding up?"

"Good." She gave him what she hoped was a confident smile. "The problem is my dad."

"Danny-boy DeMille? He's a problem solver, not the other way around." He dropped his arms and raised his eyebrows. "Is he worried about you?"

"He's overreacting, right? I'm better equipped than most people to take care of myself. I'm good with a gun and an expert in karate and other martial arts."

"Sorry, kiddo, logic doesn't apply when it comes to family." He rubbed his chin. "On the off chance we might have some clear intel that your dad would want to hear, I want you to come into this meeting with me and Mason. After that, I'll make the call."

"Thank you."

"This is as much for my benefit as yours. I don't want to lose you as the kids' nanny."

The compliment was nice to hear. She followed Prescott inside and took a seat near the end of the table beside Josh. What a jerk he was! She felt like punching him but held back. Instead, she smiled and nodded to several of the people at the table whom she'd met before when they visited the Prescotts' home in Aspen.

Sitting to the admiral's left was Hank Grossman—a slouchy, sloppy, middle-aged man with hair that looked like steel wool. Instead of waving, he pointed at her as though his fingers were a gun—a gesture that was particularly inappropriate given the circumstances. Did he mean to threaten her? Was he working with the bad guys? Lexie copied his gesture and pretended to shoot back at him. *Take that, Grossman.*

He was with the NSA. She knew his job was top secret but had no idea what he did or what his title was or anything else about him, other than he couldn't get through a meal without dribbling a smear on his necktie.

Beside Grossman was Sam Bertinelli, also NSA, who was dark with classic features and much more pleasant. He gave her a nod and a wink. His buttoned-down appearance was well suited for a junior executive, but Bertinelli was a little too old to be a junior anything. Certainly too old for her, which was basically what she'd told him when he'd asked her out on a date a few months ago. They had both been polite, but she'd seen the flare of hostility in his hazel eyes. The two NSA dudes were a little scary.

Josh's pointy woodpecker nose jabbed in her direction. "I spoke to your father."

"I'm aware," she said in a low voice oozing with sarcasm. "You made it sound like we were under assault from terrorist madmen. He's freaked."

"Odd. He's a marine. I didn't think he'd get upset."

She hated the insinuation. Her dad was tougher than nails; he could handle anything. "Are you saying that my dad is a wimp?"

"Hush, now."

"Take it back."

"Fine."

His head swiveled so he faced the head of the table. Again, he reminded her of a bird with virtually no neck and a round, soft body. Why did Prescott keep him around as an assistant? Josh was neither smart nor funny nor pleasant. He did, however, fulfill whatever he was ordered to do without question or hesitation. She supposed there was something to be said for blind obedience.

Including Josh, there were seven men seated around the table and two women, one in uniform and one in a body-hugging cocktail dress with one shoulder bare.

At the head of the table, next to the bared shoulder, was a slick, good-looking guy. He rose to his feet and buttoned the front of his tux. He wasn't as tall as Mason, who was standing behind the admiral, and he wasn't as muscular. But a lot of women would have found his sweep of glistening blond hair and brilliant blue eyes appealing. The tux helped.

She leaned toward Josh. "Who's that?"

"Robert Collier, CIA."

His voice was a bit higher than she expected and had an interesting accent. Maybe French? Lexie had gotten accustomed to these suave, international men who came to visit at the Prescott home in Aspen. She suspected Collier would be a hand kisser.

"The woman next to him," she whispered to Josh, "is also CIA?"

Josh nodded.

Apparently, Collier had been waiting for the admiral to return. He addressed the group. "In my interrogation of the four men in custody, I have learned that they are part of a group called the Anti-Conspiracy Committee for Democracy, or the AC-CD."

The name of the group didn't sound dangerous. Nobody in this room was against democracy. And who wasn't anti-conspiracy? Resting her elbow on the table, she leaned forward and focused on Collier.

He pointed to the flat screen mounted on the wall behind where she was sitting. She turned to look over her shoulder. The screen was blank. Mounted on the wall near the door was an elk head with an impressive ten-point rack. On the other side of the screen was a seriously ugly boar with curly tusks.

"I would usually have photos and a logo," he said in his lilting accent, "but the members of the very loosely organized AC-CD pride themselves on being anonymous. They meet in groups of no more than five. The head of AC-CD is referred to as the leader, and sometimes different people take that responsibility."

Bertinelli nudged the shoulder of his NSA boss as he pointed out the obvious. "For a group opposed to conspiracy, they have a lot of secrets."

"That is why," Collier said with a cold glance toward the NSA contingent, "it is complicated to compile facts and information about the AC-CD."

"How did you get them to talk?" Bertinelli asked.

"They would hardly shut up. I have never had an interrogation like this. They were eager to tell me that their job was vitally important on a global level. They all used the same words—'vital importance' and 'international repercussions' and more of those catchphrases."

He swore in French and stuck out his jaw. His icy blond hair shimmered under the overhead lights.

"Excuse me," said the uniformed woman, "but what was the job they were assigned to do?"

"To kidnap the admiral."

All eyes focused on Prescott. Unperturbed, he shrugged and said, "Then they weren't after my children. Is that correct?"

"Correct, sir."

"Or my wife."

"Just you," Collier said. "Their plan was to drug your wife's bedtime drink so she would sleep soundly. When everything was quiet, they would slip into your bedroom and abduct you. Under no circumstances were they supposed to hurt you."

"Why?" Prescott asked.

"They are searching for the Damascus Cache, and they believe you have knowledge of its whereabouts."

Prescott scoffed. "The Damascus Cache was destroyed years ago."

Beside her, Josh wriggled in his chair like a schoolboy who had the right answer to the teacher's question. She gave him a nudge. "Go ahead and speak up."

"I better not." That was why he was a woodpecker and not an eagle. To her, he whispered, "I've heard chatter. People talking about the cache."

Her cell phone buzzed. A text was coming through from Megan, the oldest Prescott kid. It said, Hurry back. The brats won't go to bed.

It was kind of amazing that Lexie had been away for as long as she had without a minor crisis or two from the children. It looked as though she'd have to wait until later to get Prescott to talk to her dad.

She stood and pointed to her phone. "Please excuse me. Duty calls. I need to go upstairs and tell some bedtime stories."

"I'll be up soon," Prescott said. "Mason, accompany her."

He was at her side so quickly that he was turning the doorknob before she could touch it. In the hallway, he closed the door and spoke into his headset.

When he was beside her, she asked, "Who were you talking to?"

"Dylan. He has cameras in the conference room so he can keep an eye on things until I get back."

"Do you need to go back?"

"Prescott asked me to stay close."

She didn't like the way that sounded. "He doesn't trust the people around him."

"Do you blame him?"

"Not really."

The men and women in that conference room were spies, spooks and feds—high-ranking members of the intelligence community. It dawned on her that she'd met several of these people. "Do you think my dad is right? Am I in danger?"

"Not right now."

As they strolled to the elevators, his vigilant attitude relaxed, and he seemed to shed his bodyguard persona. She liked being with him. And he must like her, too. He'd kissed her, after all.

She pushed the elevator button. "Should I stay with the Prescotts or should I quit?"

"Do you like your job?"

"I do. It's not a career I want for the rest of my life, but I like it."

"Are you scared?"

She thought for a moment before answering. In the bathroom upstairs, she'd had a few moments of intense panic when she'd fallen through a time warp to relive her accident. But her fear had dissipated. "I'm cautious but not frightened."

"Cautious is good," he said as they boarded the elevator. "There's no glory in taking risks."

"I don't know what to do."

The elevator doors closed. They were wrapped together in a wood-paneled cocoon. She caught a whiff of his citrusy aftershave. She slowly blinked. In her imagination, their clothes melted away. In another long blink, they twined in each other's arms. A gush of passion swept through her.

An elevator bell dinged when they hit the seventh floor, and she focused on him. He was watching her with a wary but bemused expression. "You checked out. What were you thinking?"

She stepped into the hallway outside the elevator. The teddy bear on the side table that had been gunned down earlier had already been replaced by a new stuffed animal. No way would she tell him that she'd fantasized about him. Instead, she switched direction. "You haven't answered me. Stay or go back to Texas?"

"I don't think there's a logical solution," he said. "What does your heart tell you?"

Lexie didn't usually think of things in touchy-feely terms; she wasn't raised that way. But she did have feelings about her job. Going back to her father's house felt like admitting defeat. Along that line, she wasn't one to be scared off.

Her heart also told her that she liked being part of the Prescott clan. With them, she shared intimate family moments that had never been possible with her brothers and father.

And there was one more heartfelt reason. She thought of it as she watched the two littlest Prescott kids dashing down the hallway toward her with the huge Carlos in pursuit. If she left Colorado, she would probably never see Mason again.

She turned to him and gave a decisive nod. "I'm staying."

Chapter Six

The next morning at nine o'clock, Mason climbed into the passenger side of a golf cart beside Admiral Prescott. Following an asphalt path, Prescott drove from the practice putting green toward the first tee. In normal circumstances, Mason enjoyed the game and was a couple of notches under par. From a bodyguard's perspective, he hated golf. Everybody on the course was carrying a bag filled with metal implements, providing a handy hiding place for a gun or rifle. Though Mason would be sticking tight to the admiral for close-in protection, they were surrounded by forested hills where an army of bad guys could be lurking.

The local sheriff had his deputies combing through the trees and rocks, and helicopters made occasional swoops, but there was no effective way to shield against an assault from a sniper with a long-range precision rifle. Those babies were accurate at a thousand yards.

Mason took comfort in the knowledge that the Anti-Conspiracy Committee for Democracy plan was for kidnapping and not assassination. Also, if the guys they picked up last night were any sample, the AC-CD was a committee of numskulls.

Last night he'd heard more details from CIA Agent Collier's interrogation. The AC-CD thugs had broken into the admiral's room and downloaded the contents of his computer and his wife's computer onto memory sticks. They'd readily admitted to Collier that they didn't think the admiral was careless enough to transport the Damascus Cache on his personal computer, but they needed to look everywhere.

Their kidnapping plot was foiled when Lexie showed up too early on the seventh floor. Her appearance caught them unprepared; they'd only had time to get changed and drag a couple of the real guards into a vacant room to hide their unconscious bodies. The real guards had been zapped by stun guns and none of them were seriously injured. The only person to require an ambulance was the guy Lexie had karate kicked into dreamland.

The thought of the petite, auburn-haired nanny beating up an armed bad guy brought a smile to Mason's face. This mental image of Lexie was a pleasant distraction. Behind his sunglasses, he kept his eyes in motion, scanning the hillsides, anticipating threats before they became real.

"I'm glad you and your men are here," Prescott said.

"You're the boss. We'll stay as long as you want."

"Good to know." He checked his wristwatch. "In about an hour, I'll need to pull away from the rest of the foursome and take a meeting on the computer."

"A face-to-face meeting?"

"Yes, your partner Dylan set it up for me. He says all I have to do is turn on the laptop and push one button."

"I'll make sure the meeting stays private." Mason glanced over at Prescott. His close-cropped white hair was covered by a dark blue cap with *NAVY* written in gold. He was tanned and looked healthy in khakis and a lightweight gray sweater. "Lexie said you were keeping TST around because you don't trust these other guys."

"She's a very perceptive young woman—her father's daughter." Prescott frowned. "My conversation with him last night could have gone better. I get it. The man is concerned. Hell, I'd feel the same way if one of my kids had been attacked. But I believe these idiots were after me, not the nanny or Helena or the children. They should all be safe."

"What did her father say to her?"

"He was willing to have Lexie stay."

And that was fortunate, because she'd already made up her mind about what she intended to do. "Do you mind if I ask a personal question?"

"Go ahead."

Mason cleared his throat. "Is Lexie dating anyone?"

"When she first came to us, she asked about a boyfriend by the name of Anton. But she's forgotten him. And she's only gone out on a couple of dates." He gave a sly grin. "Any other questions?"

"When is her next day off?"

MASON ACCOMPANIED THE FOURSOME: Prescott, Collier and the two NSA guys—Hank Grossman and Sam Bertinelli. Predictably, Collier was a superb golfer with picture-perfect form. Bertinelli wasn't half bad, but took way too long to set up each shot, testing the wind direction and picking bits of grass out of the way. The admiral played solid, par-level golf. And Grossman cheated.

Since they were zipping around in golf carts, the only chance for conversation was on the green. Collier, Prescott and Bertinelli followed golf etiquette and kept their voices low so they wouldn't disturb the putter. Grossman wasn't so polite.

"Listen up, boys," Grossman growled. Mason guessed that the gray-haired, stoop-shouldered man was older than the admiral, definitely north of sixty. "Let's take advantage of this time alone to talk about the Damascus Cache. We all know what it is. Don't pretend that you don't."

"I've heard talk," Prescott said, "about a comprehensive list of personnel and weapons in the Middle East and sub-Saharan Africa. A cache of information, compiled several years ago at the end of the Bush administration."

"More valuable than a cache of gold," Grossman said.

"Not all of it." Prescott's ball was in a bunker, farthest from the hole. Therefore, he was first to shoot. After selecting a wedge club, he positioned his feet in the sand, straightened his shoulders, glanced at the flag and hit a perfect chip shot. The ball stopped a mere six inches from the hole.

As he tapped his ball into the cup, he continued, "There were lists of supplies, locations of arsenals and maps of supply lines. At least, I'd guess the cache included that information—details that are now worthless."

"It is about the people," Collier said.

The next to putt was Bertinelli. His ball was about thirty-five feet from the hole, and Mason guessed it was going to take five minutes for Bertinelli to test the wind and tamp down divots. A waste of time—this average golfer wasn't going to make such a long putt.

"I agree about the danger posed to the people on this list," said Prescott. "I'm not saying that I've ever seen the cache or that I even know it exists, but I'd guess that it would give details about intelligence operatives for the military, the CIA, NSA and Interpol. Many were undercover."

"Many still are," Collier said. "These are people who may or may not still be involved in espionage. Some have dropped off the grid and are leading normal lives. They are married. They have children."

"Ha!" Grossman exploded with a loud, humorless laugh. "I'm guessing that these former spies sure as hell don't want their names made public."

"Exposure would be a death warrant."

Finally in position over the ball, Bertinelli looked confused. "Why would AC-CD want the list?"

"Hurry up and putt," Grossman said. "As for the AC-CD, they claim to be anti-conspiracy. So they might think they're doing the world a favor by causing trouble for spies."

"An altruistic motive," Prescott said.

"Yeah, yeah, they're shining a light on the truth. That kind of phony-baloney."

Mason pinched his lips together to keep from blurting out his ideas and opinions. His college degree was in international relations. Because his brother had been stationed in the Middle East, he'd focused on that area and on Africa. These were lands where espionage ran rampant, lands where bribes were more common than taxes, lands of genocide. Heinous battles were motivated by politics, religion, ethnicity and plain old greed. He seriously doubted that AC-CD wanted the Damascus Cache to expose the truth.

Bertinelli tapped his ball. It traveled slowly but steadily and…plink! He sank the putt and gave a victorious arm pump. This guy wasn't the sharpest tool in the shed, but he shouldn't be counted out.

"I got the answer," Grossman said. "Destroy the damn list. Delete it from all servers. Encrypt the hell out of it."

While he babbled about how they could destroy the cache, he misfired on a four-foot putt. His ball was about as far from the hole as Collier's, which was good enough for Grossman. He scooped it off the green and into his pocket. "That's a gimme."

Collier spoke in his smooth, lightly accented voice as he lined up his putt. "We cannot destroy something that we do not have. The Damascus Cache, whether it exists or not, is nowhere to be found."

The stroke of his putter was as elegant as his tailored black trousers and cashmere sweater. When the ball dropped into the hole, he casually removed his sunglasses. His blue-eyed gaze zeroed in on Prescott. "I wonder, Admiral, why do these people believe that you are in possession of the cache?"

"A damned good question," Grossman bellowed. "I know you worked in intelligence with the navy SEALs, but you're retired."

Not to be left out, Bertinelli added his two cents. "You're a surprising target, sir. You have a reputation for not being comfortable with computer technology."

"True," Prescott said. "I still have trouble figuring out how to make my phone send texts."

"Why you?" Collier repeated.

The admiral didn't even attempt to answer. He shrugged, checked his wristwatch and started walking toward their cart. "Play the next hole without me. I'll catch up after I take a meeting."

"We're going to miss you," Grossman called after him.

"I'll bet."

The admiral drove the cart toward a grove of aspens that were several yards off the fairway. Apparently, he wanted privacy for this meeting. Not only did he put distance between them and the others in the foursome, but the outdoor location made it difficult for anyone else to overhear. Mason knew that his buddy Dylan would have set up a computerized meeting that was nearly impossible to hack.

"I need you to keep time," Prescott said as he handed Mason the Luminox wristwatch preferred by the SEALs. "I need to log on at precisely 10:44 and log off at 10:59."

Mason took the watch. Three minutes until log-on. The admiral had the computer open on his lap. He flexed his fingers and cleared his throat. And then…

"Trouble approaching," Mason said.

A golf cart with a distinctive pink top bounced across the fairway toward them. In the driver's seat, Helena hunched over the steering wheel like a speed racer and squealed wildly on every bump. Riding shotgun, Lexie clung to the fringed pink top and laughed.

The admiral shook his head and grinned. "That's my woman."

A lot of men, especially those in positions of authority, would have been annoyed by Helena's wild driving, but Prescott was amused, even a little bit proud of his flamboyant wife.

"Sir." Mason tapped the face of the watch. "It's time."

Prescott touched the correct computer key, and the laptop screen showed a broad-shouldered man sitting at a desk. His face was easily recognizable from television talk shows—a lantern jaw, heavy brows and thick black hair with silver streaks at the temple. He was the Secretary of the Navy, Thomas Benson.

"Good morning," Prescott said.

"Maybe where you are it's morning." Benson's jaw lifted, and he scowled into the screen. "Here at the Pentagon it's past my feeding time. What's happening, Prescott? Tell me about these anti-conspiracy whack jobs."

"Not much to tell," he replied. "My concern is the Damascus Cache. I thought we'd destroyed every copy."

Mason took note of the change in Prescott's attitude. With the other golfers, he'd been cagey about whether or not the Damascus Cache even existed. While he was talking to the SecNav, a veteran officer who was a peer and an equal, there was a total lack of pretense. These two spoke truth to each other.

The SecNav shook his head. "I can't be certain that one copy didn't get away from us."

"Who was responsible for getting rid of this intelligence?"

"Your old buddy, Al Ackerman."

"I was afraid you'd say that."

With one last squeal, Helena parked next to them in the shadow of the aspens. She bounded from the cart and came around so she could see over her husband's shoulder. The instant she recognized the man on the screen, she fluttered her fingertips in a wave. "Hello there, Tommy."

"Helena." His smile was so broad it looked as if his jaw would unhinge. "Lovely as ever, and who's that with you?"

"Our nanny, Lexie DeMille," she said as she dragged Lexie into the camera range.

Mason noticed how Lexie's posture went from relaxed to as stiff as steel rebar, almost as though she was standing at attention. He understood why she straightened up. No matter where she went or what she became, Lexie was a military brat. SecNav was a man of the highest rank and authority.

"It's a pleasure to meet you, sir," she said with a slight quaver in her voice.

Prescott said, "She's Danny DeMille's daughter. As long as I'm making introductions, my bodyguard is Mason Steele. His brother was Matthew."

To his amazement, the SecNav saluted him. "Matthew Steele was a hero. His quick thinking saved thirty-seven children. My condolences to you and to your parents."

"Thank you, sir."

Mason was reeling. The SecNav knew his brother. More than that, he knew something about the circumstances of Matthew's death. He had posthumously been awarded a Purple Heart, his second such award, so his family had known that he'd died honorably. Still, hearing the details would mean a great deal to Mason's parents.

With a start, he realized that Prescott was talking to him, telling him to move the ladies out of the way while he finished his conversation. Mason herded Lexie and Helena deeper into the aspen grove while leaving a clear route back to the admiral in case he needed to get back there in a hurry.

"Wow," Lexie said. "Thomas Benson knows who my dad is. I can't believe it! And I met him, too."

"He's just good old Tommy," Helena said. "The man is a sweetheart and a ham. Did you know that he was a pilot?"

Both Mason and Lexie nodded. Though he was interested in her story, he kept one eye on Prescott. Mason was curious about the "old buddy" named Ackerman. Why had the admiral expressed concern when the SecNav mentioned him?

"At a karaoke bar in DC," Helena continued, "Tommy and Prescott serenaded me. Can you guess what they sang?"

Lexie nodded. "The SecNav was a top gun. I'm guessing they sang 'You've Lost That Lovin' Feelin'.'"

"Of course, you're right."

Helena started singing, and Lexie backed her up. Damn, they were cheerful. If he hadn't known better, he wouldn't have believed that Lexie had recently been in a firefight and Helena's husband was under threat of abduction. Was the singing and smiling a front? Showing a brave face so the kids wouldn't be scared?

He took a long moment to study Lexie. Her black jeans fit smoothly. On the top, she wore a white shirt with an eyelet trim under an embroidered denim jacket. Once again, her curly hair was yanked up in a high ponytail. He liked the casual version of Lexie. If she was faking this carefree attitude, he'd have to nominate her for an award.

Prescott motioned for them to join him as he powered down the laptop and closed it. Still singing and snapping her fingers, Helena approached him and kissed both cheeks, leaving a scarlet imprint of lipstick.

"Are we okay?" she asked.

"We're fine," he assured her. "But I'm going to need to spend another day or two at the Pentagon next week."

"Next week is the start of our summer schedule. We're all taking off in different directions, and I want to get packed and organized."

Prescott looked around her shoulder to make eye contact with Lexie. "How about it—are you ready to organize the Prescott troops?"

"Ready to try," she said.

"How's the arm?"

"Doesn't hurt a bit. At the worst, I'll have another scar to add to my collection."

Mason had wanted to ask the same thing. What did she mean about a collection of scars? There was so much more he wanted to know about her.

Prescott took on a serious expression. "I want to promise you, Lexie, that we will find and destroy any existing copies of the Damascus Cache. But I know better than to make guarantees that cannot be fulfilled with certainty."

"I'm sure you'll do your best." Her lips twisted in a confused smile. "But I'm not sure why this would be important to me."

"The cache is a list of undercover operatives in the Middle East. It was generated several years ago." He took her hand and squeezed. "Your father's name is on it."

Chapter Seven

Tony Curtis blended in with the valets handling parking at the boutique hotel. He'd grabbed a uniform—a black vest and a bolo tie—from the garage, and he found a name tag in the top drawer of a beat-up desk by the lockers. The name was Andy. Not entirely accurate, but close enough. He sidled up the drive to the desk at the front entrance, where guests were checking out and demanding their vehicles.

Though he was probably fifteen years older than the other valets, his build was as lean and wiry as an eighteen-year-old's, and he'd plucked the few gray hairs from his thick black mane. It was no problem for him to pass himself off as a young dude with a hard-luck story.

Along with the rest of the crew, he hustled back and forth to the underground parking to retrieve the Escalades, Bimmers and Hummers. He let the other guys do most of the work. They didn't care. This was a job that ran on tips.

Tony made no effort to be secretive or to hide. Instead, he acted as if he belonged. He played his role as a guy who was too old to be making a living as a valet…doing it anyway but not even trying to do it well.

A job like this might have been his really real life. He smirked at the thought, acknowledging that the person who had babbled about really real life was Franny, who now wanted to be called Lexie. Hell, why not? Lexie rhymed with sexy, and that suited her. She was hot, sexier now than when he'd known her. He was almost glad he hadn't killed her.

What set him apart from the other valets was his intense training with firearms and his instinct for murder. In the past few moments, he'd been tempted to lash out. Taking gratuities made him feel like a servant. When a pompous, red-faced rich man dribbled a one-dollar bill into Tony's outstretched hand and stood waiting for a "thank you, sir," a homicidal urge boiled up inside the not-really-a-valet.

Since metal detectors were all over the hotel, he hadn't hidden a gun up his sleeve. Nor was he carrying the well-honed hunting knife he used to gut and clean a deer in five minutes. Tony had two weapons strapped to his chest under his vest. One was a stun gun. The other was a razor-sharp plastic chef's blade.

He locked gazes with the pompous hotel guest. Tony could kill this fool in ways that didn't require a weapon. With a deft twist, he could snap the rich man's neck. Eye gouging was an option. Or a quick, lethal chop to the trachea.

The rich man must have recognized Tony's deeper nature, because he peeled off a ten to accompany the one-dollar bill, quickly dived behind the steering wheel of his shiny SUV and drove away.

Nobody paid any attention when Tony edged around to the side of the hotel and pulled out a cigarette. From this vantage point, he could see the admiral and his buddies playing golf. Life would have been so much easier if he could have just killed the admiral. The kidnapping scheme meant the admiral had to be incapacitated and then removed from the scene. Neither would happen while the bodyguard protected him.

Tony traced the edge of the leather knife sheath fastened to his chest. He came to the conclusion that the only way to abduct the admiral required killing the bodyguard.

THOUGH THE DAY was sunny and clear, Lexie felt cold shadows closing around her, tweaking her shoulders and sending shivers down her spine. Standing on the balcony outside her hotel room, she stared into the warm blue Colorado sky and thought about Texas, the closest place she had to a home. Like most military families, the DeMilles had moved from base to base around the country while her parents were together. After the split, she and her brothers had been raised by her grandma in Austin while her dad was stationed far away. And working as a spy?

She hadn't even known that the marines had spies, but of course they did. Every branch of the military had intelligence officers, and the SEALs were totally involved in undercover ops. Still, she didn't think of her dad as a secret agent. How could that be? Suave wasn't part of his vocabulary. He was loud, demanding and straightforward…just about as subtle as a charging Brahman bull.

But the SecNav and Admiral Prescott wouldn't lie to her. According to those two, Danny DeMille was not only a spy, but in danger of being outed by something called the Damascus Cache. What could she do? How was she going to keep her dad safe?

The smartest move would be to rush home, throw a fence around him and shoot anybody who got too close. As if he'd put up with that? His lifestyle didn't exactly lend itself to the efforts of a bodyguard. Why couldn't he be a typical retired dad who stayed at home and puttered and watched football on TV?

When he'd left the marines and come home to nurse her back to health, she felt bad about making him change his whole life. He confided that being a soldier hadn't been his number one choice, anyway. His cherished goal in life was to be a cowboy. After she was mostly recovered, he made his dream become really real when he found a job with a buddy who owned a dude ranch. The work suited him. Her dad was the Marlboro Man without the cigarettes.

She heard a rap on the door and turned. "Come in."

Mason pushed open the door. She hadn't expected to see him again but was glad he'd shown up. Last night, she'd experienced a wonderful, luscious sleep filled with X-rated fantasies about this tall, muscular man with the sky blue eyes and the buzz-cut hair. Whether her dreams were a result of the pain pills the hotel doctor had given her or came from a deeper need, she hadn't wanted to wake up this morning.

With his hand on the knob, he stood framed in her doorway like a cover photo. He looked great in his khaki trousers, collared shirt and the dark blue sports jacket he wore to cover his gun holster. And what would she call this portrait? Casual stud? Golfing bodyguard? Husky, handsome hunk?

She cleared her throat. "Are you done with your golf round?"

"Prescott only played the front nine. He wanted to come back here and talk to Helena before she took off with you and the kids."

"So you left the two of them—the admiral and his wife—alone in their bedroom suite," she said. "Is that proper bodyguard procedure?"

"Not really." With the door to Lexie's room still open, he turned his head and looked down the hall toward the suite. "I should be right outside his door, but I wanted to catch you before you left."

She truly enjoyed hearing those words. The chill of fear that had been poking at her melted a bit. Mason warmed her in many different ways. She floated across the room, stood beside him and whispered, "What did you want to say to me?"

"Prescott said you'd talked to your dad. Are you going back to Austin?"

The apprehensions that had been momentarily swept aside surged to the forefront of her mind. "Do you think I should?"

"If you're scared, my answer is yes." Parallel lines

creased his forehead as he considered. "However, I don't think you need to feel nervous or afraid. The AC-CD is after the admiral, and he's planning to fly straight to the Pentagon after one more round of golf with big donors."

"Hold on there. He's supposed to return to the house with us." She followed Mason's glance toward the suite. "Oh, I see. He's trying to explain. I don't think Helena expected him to go to the Pentagon so soon. He's retired, supposedly."

"He mentioned that I might want to protect him from her."

"Indeed," she said.

Helena had a temper, and she'd be plenty angry that her husband was escaping the hectic hassle of getting ready for the summer season. During the next few days, the kids would be taking off in different directions for different projects. Even Helena was busy—scheduled to be filming in Toronto.

"The admiral has to fend for himself when it comes to his wild and crazy wife," Mason said. "I'm worried about you."

"Me?" She pulled one fist to her waist and thrust the other forward in a karate pose. "I can take care of myself."

"You are wise, Lexie-*san*. Not going back to Texas?"

"I didn't say that." She dropped the pose. "I'm nervous about my father being named in the Damascus Cache. He's done so much for me. He stayed with me when I thought I was going to die. At the very least, I should run home and watch his back."

"I thought you had brothers in Austin."

"I do." Unfortunately, contacting her brothers and telling them about the threat wasn't possible. The admiral had made her promise not to tell anyone else. "The Damascus Cache is top secret."

"Right."

"I could try to convince my dad to go into hiding. Maybe he'd qualify for witness protection."

She seriously doubted that he'd agree to any form of protection, even if it made sense. Whether he was wearing his dress blue uniform or riding the range in his favorite Stetson, her dad was a manly man. He believed in uncommon valor and never ran from a fight.

"Best-case scenario," Mason said, "Prescott locates the existing copy of the cache—if there is such a thing—and he destroys it."

She didn't understand why it should be the admiral's job to deal with the cache. He was retired. Why didn't the AC-CD understand that? Why had they come after Prescott? And why wasn't she taking this conversation with Mason to a more interesting place? "Enough about my dad."

"Talking about him is important. If you leave to watch over him, I have to drive over nine hundred miles to take you out to dinner."

"And if I don't go?"

"It's a mere two hundred miles from Denver to Aspen. When's your next day off?"

"Thursday," she said quickly. In her mind, that date was lit up in neon party colors. Five days from now on

Thursday, the Prescott family would be pursuing their summer adventures. She'd have the house to herself.

"I'll pick you up at five." With most guys, hand kisses were smarmy. Not Mason. He lifted her hand and lightly pressed his full lips against her knuckles. The resulting angle of her arm was a bit uncomfortable. She winced.

"Does it hurt?" he asked. "The bullet wound?"

"I hardly feel it." There were light twinges when she moved her arm a certain way, and she intended to baby herself for a couple of days—not lifting children or carrying luggage.

"What did you mean when you said it was another scar for your collection?"

"I was in a car accident. Operations on both legs left some interesting marks, and I've got a couple of surgical scars on my abdomen."

"That sounds serious."

"A hit-and-run," she said dismissively. Her accident was definitely *not* something she wanted to talk about. Instead, she concentrated on the fun she'd have going out with Mason. "Where should we eat?"

"Do you like German?"

"Ja, ich liebe Strudel."

"You love strudel. Me, too." He chuckled. "Tell me more about this car accident. How old were you?"

"Fresh out of college." She shook her head. No more about the accident. "Five o'clock is an early start for a date."

"We'll have a couple of German beers before we

eat." He cocked his head to one side. "I want to hear more about this accident."

"There's not much to say. Another car clipped my fender. I lost control and drove my brother's car over a cliff. While I was crashing, I was more scared about how mad he'd be that I broke his car."

"And was he?"

The familiar ache crept over her. Her brothers had been only concerned about her. In fact, the one whose car she'd been driving blamed himself for not having a safer vehicle. "You know, Mason, I don't want to talk about the accident. I should have died, but I didn't. That's all."

He gently glided his hand down her uninjured arm and held her hand. "You don't mind having another scar?"

"Not from a bullet wound." She lifted her chin and looked up at him. "It's kinda cool. That's what the kids say."

"The twins caught a glimpse of you doing a flying kick on the armed man outside the elevator. Impressive move!"

"Yeah, they think I'm awesome until the next time I tell them they can't drink a gallon of their favorite high-octane energy drink before bed." She knew it wouldn't take long for the kids to slot her back into the boring-nanny category.

"Kids keep you grounded. The Prescott gang doesn't care that their father is an international consultant. Mom is a movie star? So what?"

Those were perceptive observations for a guy who

was essentially an only child and didn't have regular contact with children. "How come you're not a daddy?"

"I haven't found the right mommy." Still holding her hand, he pivoted slightly to face her. His gaze bored into hers. "I wouldn't mind settling down and having a family. Not that I'm looking…"

But he was, she could tell. She felt him peering into her eyes, trying to discover a sign that she was the one he was looking for. Could she be the right mommy for his children?

Part of her wanted to fling herself into his arms and tell him that she was the one. *Yes, pick me.* But motherhood wasn't in her future. It was cruel to lead him on. Dating her would be a waste of his time.

Before she could say anything, the door to the Prescott suite opened and the admiral stepped out. His gray sweater was askew. He was carrying his hat and his shoes. Helena appeared in the doorway behind him, wearing a sultry smile and a filmy black negligee with a feather trim that made it over-the-top.

Mason whispered, "Looks like they're done fighting."

"And have moved on to makeup sex." Lexie was familiar with this pattern. Passionate arguments followed by what she could only assume was equally passionate lovemaking was typical. "Here's what's strange about the movie star/love goddess. She's kind of a prude."

"Hmm." Mason wasn't actually drooling, but was clearly mesmerized by the voluptuous body under the sheer black fabric. "You don't say."

"But I do." She pulled her hand back and punched

his arm. "Here's how Helena rolls. After marriage, anything goes. But she won't allow unmarried couples to sleep in the same bedroom in her house. That might explain why she's been married five times."

"Probably," he agreed.

Prescott waved to him as he stuck his toe into his right shoe. "Let's go, Mason."

"Apparently, we're done playing golf. The admiral isn't wearing his spiked golf shoes, just sneakers." He took a step away from her. "There's another alternative—something else you could do about your dad."

She followed him, taking two steps in his direction. "What is it?"

"Do you remember how I said this could all be over if the admiral found copies of the cache and destroyed them?"

"Yes." Of course she remembered. It had only been a few minutes ago.

"Admiral Prescott isn't the only one who has access. I'll bet you've overheard more top secret intelligence than most high-clearance agents are told."

"Me?" Her voice was a squeak. "You think I could figure this out?"

"It's better than sitting around doing nothing."

As Mason hustled down the hall to the admiral's side, she watched his retreating form. She liked the breadth of his shoulders and his athletic stride. If she'd had a clear view of his bottom under his jacket, she probably would have liked that, too. More than anything, she appreciated the way his mind worked.

Someone had to locate the mysterious Damascus

Cache. Why not her? Mason was correct when he said that she'd overheard a lot of high-level intelligence. Most people didn't pay much attention to the nanny. She'd have to put it all together and figure it out. She was good at puzzles. The solution couldn't be that complicated. She could do it.

Her father had devoted much of his life to protecting his home and country. He had always kept her safe. Now it was her turn.

Find the cache. Save her dad.

Chapter Eight

Given her new agenda about searching for and ultimately destroying the Damascus Cache, Lexie looked
forward to the fifty-minute drive from the hotel to the
family's home near Aspen. She'd have a chance to talk
with Helena and get the inside scoop. No matter how
much Lexie had overheard during the last couple of
days, those meetings, discussions and consultations
weren't the same as private conversations.

The admiral often chose to confide the most important details to his wife. He didn't blab about troop
movements or spy craft or undercover operations, but
he told her the human stories—the incidents that af-
fected his heart.

More than once this morning, Lexie had noticed
Helena studying her with a goopy, sympathetic expression on her beautiful face. Neither of the Prescotts was
the sort of person who treated the nanny like a piece
of furniture, but they weren't all buddy-buddy. Lexie's
wild ride across the golf course with Helena was an
exception to the rule. They were always friendly, but

didn't hug each other every five minutes, which was exactly the way Lexie liked it.

How come Helena kept looking at her and exhaling a massive, dramatic sigh? What did she know? And how could Lexie get the admiral's wife to open up? There were a lot of distractions, but that was inescapable with six children.

At the front of the hotel, the kids fought about who got to sit where. Lexie moved closer to Helena, watching as the hotel porters loaded suitcases into the back of the second SUV.

"Ridiculous," Helena murmured. "We have too much stuff."

"No way around the baggage," Lexie said. "Including me, there are suitcases for ten people. Six kids, you and the admiral, plus me and Josh."

"Some days, it feels like all we do is pack and unpack."

"So true." Impatiently, Lexie waited for the right moment when she could change the topic from luggage to espionage.

"I told Josh he couldn't ride with us."

"Good." Let the woodpecker use his own car. "What about the admiral?"

"Edgar will be taking a chopper. Top Gun Tommy decided that my husband needs military protection, so he has a couple of stiff-neck men in uniform tromping along behind him."

Lexie didn't bother correcting her about the top gun status; the SecNav ranked way higher than that. But she had another concern. If Prescott had military bodyguards, he didn't need TST Security, which meant that Mason wouldn't be coming back to the house with them. Damn it, she missed him already. "What are the driving arrangements for you and me?"

"You drive the car in front with the older kids, and I'll take this one with the twins and the babies, and I'll use a driver from the hotel."

Lexie had wanted time alone with Helena, but that wasn't going to happen on this ride with only the two of them to handle all the kids. Later she'd find a time for a private talk with Helena.

The twins positioned themselves on either side of Lexie. Caine rested his shaggy blond head against her shoulder. "I want to ride with you."

Shane did the same with the opposite shoulder. "I want you to protect us."

"What about me?" their mother asked. "I'm a straight shooter, and I'm great at hand-to-hand combat."

"In the movies," the twins said together.

The oldest boy, Edgar Jr., popped into the conversation. "I'm almost old enough to drive. I could use the practice."

"I don't think so," Helena said.

Lexie knew what was going on with the kids. They were swarming, taking advantage of their mom being tired and a little bit frazzled. It was time for Lexie to turn into Bossy Nanny and take charge. She shook off the clingy twins.

Her first order was directed at them. "Shane and Caine, take your little brother and sister and put them in the car seats in the back SUV. You will also ride in that car."

"With you?"

"With your mom and a driver from the hotel." She made a quick pivot and pointed to the oldest girl. "Meggie, you ride with me and Eddy in the second car."

Eddy beamed, and she could see the beginning of a resemblance between the teenager and his father. "I get to drive."

"If you're really good, I'll take you out later. For practice."

"No fair. Meg gets to drive all the time."

"She's a year and a half older than you."

"But I need to drive."

Meggie said, "And I want to ride with Justin."

"Who?"

"The driver from the hotel."

Lexie was sympathetic when it came to Meggie and her potential boyfriends. The young man in question seemed polite, clean and he was a local with a job. She nodded to Meggie. "I think I can change the seating arrangements."

"You're the best."

She took over the rest of the preparations for departure, instructing the hotel staff on where to put the suitcases and herding the kids and their mother into the cars. She went to the head valet to get the keys.

There was no need to tip; Helena had given the concierge a huge gratuity to cover their departure. Lexie could tell from the giant grin on the valet's face that he was aware of the bonanza tip that would be his. He gushed over his goodbye and added, "Hope you enjoyed your stay."

She was about to make a snarky comment about how it was hard to enjoy herself when she was being shot at. Then she caught a glimpse of another one of the valets. Tall and lean with curly black hair, he was walking away from her. There was something familiar about the way he moved. Before she could ask his name, Mason rushed up beside her.

He spun her around to face him. "Thursday night at five."

"If there's a problem, I have your phone number."

"No problems." His blue eyes commanded her attention. "I'm not going to let you slip out of my life."

Her defenses went up, and the smile froze on her lips. She wanted to tell him that she wasn't part of his life, they weren't in a relationship and she was the one who decided whether she was staying or slipping. But the kids were bouncing in the cars. Little faces pressed against the windows. She had to go.

"Thursday," she said.

He ran back into the hotel, and she trotted around the two SUVs. Her mind flashed back to that valet. Someone she knew? Surely not one of the guests. But he might have been a server at the banquet. She shrugged off the vague impression.

The final arrangement in the cars put Meggie and Eddy, Jr. and the twins in the second vehicle. Lexie was driving the lead car with Helena in the passenger seat, which was exactly what she'd wanted. The two youngest were in the rear in their car seats. She started up the engine and turned to Helena.

Her gleaming black hair tumbled loosely to her shoulders as she covered her green eyes with sunglasses. Lexie knew for a fact that Helena had gotten up with the kids, had breakfast, chased after her husband with a golf cart and made love. But she still managed to look like a movie star in her leopard-patterned Windbreaker and skinny black jeans with strappy platform heels. Considering her gorgeous appearance, Helena spent remarkably little time fussing with her hair and makeup.

"It's hard to believe," Helena said, "that you don't have special training as a nanny. You're quite effective at getting everyone organized."

"That's how I was brought up. I had three older brothers and we were a handful. Organization was essential. I learned spit and polish from my Marine Corps dad."

Helena exhaled another dramatic sigh. "Your dear, sweet father."

"Clearly, you don't know my dad." He was seldom described as "dear" or "sweet."

"Edgar told me all about him. He's a good man. When you were hurt in that terrible car crash, your father came home to take care of you. He taught you to walk again."

Though she could have argued that it was her own strength of character and—as her dad readily admitted— her own damned cussedness that got her back on her feet, she agreed. Her father was a truly good man. Sometimes he was overprotective with "Daddy's baby girl," and other times he was a total hard-ass. But he was a decent human being who had done right by her. Her question was: Why were the admiral and Helena talking about Danny DeMille?

She gazed through the windshield at the beautiful spring day. The gleaming white cap of snow on Mount Sopris stood out against the clear blue sky. Fresh green buffalo grass and bright wildflowers in red, blue and yellow covered the fields. She'd miss the mountains if she had to go back to Texas.

Lexie asked, "What else did your husband say about my dad?"

"They worked together in the Middle East. They were both in attendance at Al Ackerman's wedding to that Saudi princess."

Her dad never mentioned a Saudi wedding. She was beginning to think she didn't know the man at all. "Anything else?"

"I know what you're doing, Lexie." Helena adjusted her seat belt across her breasts and glanced into the back, checking on the kids. The two little ones would quickly fall asleep in their car seats. "You're probing me to get information about the Damascus Cache."

"You got me. There's no way I can trick you into telling me everything you know. You're an actress, a good one. If you decided to stonewall or fake me out, you could easily play those roles." And Lexie couldn't compete. She was a terrible liar, incapable of manipulating. "If you don't want to talk to me, you don't have to. But I'm going to lay my cards on the table."

"Go ahead."

"Before yesterday, I'd never heard of the Damascus Cache. Then your husband was targeted for kidnapping because of it. And then I find out that my dad's name is on it. He's in danger." She caught Helena's gaze and stared hard for a second before turning back to the road. "I want to do whatever I can to find the list and destroy it."

"How can I help?"

"Tell me what you know."

"Oh, dear, where should I start?" Helena twisted a strand of ebony hair around her finger and stared out the window.

"At the beginning."

"The first time I met Edgar was in Paris. He wore a tuxedo, not a uniform, and he seemed to know everyone. He spoke fluent French, German and Japanese. And when he took me in his arms to dance the tango…"

Her voice took on a resonant, lilting tone. Helena made her real life sound like a romantic movie with perfect moonlight and fragrant gardens and a beautiful couple falling deeply and passionately in love at first sight. Lexie had heard this story before and didn't mind hearing it again.

In this retelling, Helena ended her story with an unexpected twist. "To summarize, I knew Edgar was a spy before I realized he was an admiral."

"Wow." Lexie stared through the windshield at the two-lane road that stretched before them. She knew that Prescott had worked with navy intelligence in the Middle East and western Africa, but she'd never thought of him as a spy. "Why haven't I heard this before?"

"My dah-ling Edgar wouldn't be much of a spy if everybody knew about it. And he doesn't participate in an active way. Not anymore."

"Not until this stuff with the Damascus Cache."

"Ah, the cache," Helena said. "I don't have many details."

"That's fine. Simplified works best for me."

"At one time, years ago, Edgar was one of the authors of the Damascus Cache. It contained information about supply lines, weapons, contractors and undercover contacts. The names listed represented all the various groups from the military to the CIA to MI6 to Mossad and Interpol."

"It sounds like a large document. Did they reduce it down to a flash drive?"

"Indeed, there were several copies. Here's what Sec-Nav told Edgar." She leaned across the console and whispered, "These crazy anti-conspiracy people think Edgar has hidden the cache."

"Where? At the house?"

"Apparently."

The Prescott home was twelve bedrooms on seven acres. Though the setting was secluded, the house was a hive of activity. For the past two weeks, the entire family had been in residence, which was an unusual synchronizing of schedules for a movie star, an international consultant and six active children.

The idea of searching that sprawling house for something as tiny as a flash drive was daunting. Not to mention the barn for the horses and the outbuildings. Lexie had lost pairs of shoes and pillows and notebooks that had never been found.

"Here's what I don't understand," she said. "If the cache is at the house, why come after him at this event?"

Helena shrugged. "This is where it starts getting complicated. They might have already searched the house. Probably they have. There's evidence that someone sneaked into Edgar's office and the town house in DC."

"Wait a sec. Are you saying that these AC-CD people have broken into the house in Aspen? Where we have intense electronic security and lots of people milling around?"

In addition to the family, there was a cook, a housekeeper and a couple of assistants like Josh. Also, the Prescotts did a lot of entertaining and had frequent houseguests. Lexie thought of all the people who came and went: groundskeepers, wranglers for weekends when they had horses, maids, delivery guys who handled groceries, firewood, dry cleaning and late-night pizza. Then there was Helena's staff, including a personal trainer and her hair and makeup people.

"Maybe they joined the parade of people who are always coming through." She chuckled.

"Their search of the house failed," Lexie said. "Then, their plan was to kidnap your husband. Not a clever scheme. Admiral Prescott would never give up classified information."

"Of course not. Nor would you."

"Not a chance."

"You're very brave, Lexie. That's something else you learned from your father."

Why did Helena bring up her father again? She'd delivered an important nugget of information by telling Lexie that the cache might be hidden at the house. But what else? "Is there something I'm missing? Something about my dad?"

"As an actress, I like to observe characters and character traits. Your father fascinates me. What happens when a dedicated military man is faced with trouble at home?"

"You mean when he came home to take care of me." She'd wondered about that, too. "I never understood why he retired. He could have taken a leave and then returned to active duty."

"Guilt stopped him. Your father blamed himself for what happened to you. He would never leave you unprotected again." She smiled and gently patted Lexie's arm. "When you came to work for us, he made Edgar promise on his life that he'd take care of you."

"Why would Dad feel guilty? It was my fault. I should have done more to avoid the car that hit me."

"It wasn't an accident, Lexie. The car that hit you was sending a message to the entire espionage community. If your father and my husband didn't cooperate and turn over the information they wanted, people would die."

Starting with me. Lexie's sense of what was really real had just adjusted a few notches. Someone had tried to kill her and had almost succeeded.

Helena continued, "We'll understand if you want to go back to Texas."

She'd never give up. "I'm staying."

Chapter Nine

Alone, at last! On Thursday at noon, Lexie perched on a stool at the marble-topped counter in the kitchen and savored a mug of free-trade coffee from Colombia. The stillness was pure luxury. Her eyelids lowered and lifted in a slow blink as her breathing regulated to a less frantic pace. Ever since the Prescotts had returned from the hotel on Sunday afternoon, she'd been running in high gear, racing madly to prepare the family for their summer activities.

Her lazy gaze slid around the huge French country-style kitchen with quaint white cabinets, double-sized stainless steel appliances and gobs of gadgets neatly arrayed on marble countertops. The curtains and trim were slate blue. French doors opened onto a huge cedar deck, which was perfect for entertaining and offered a wide view of Henscratch Valley, where three small rivulets combined into one wide creek that flowed into the Roaring Fork River. From a bird's-eye view, the joining of the rivulets resembled a hen's claw. Hence, the name Henscratch.

Though the Prescotts employed a cook for entertaining, grocery shopping and those occasions when Helena was on a special diet, Lexie or one of the other adults usually cooked for the family. Lexie was teaching the older kids how to make basic survival food, not that these youngsters would ever need to survive on omelets and ramen noodles. At present, the kitchen was well stocked, thanks to a massive shopping trip by the cook, who was taking a month off...as was the housekeeper.

Lexie swung around on her stool and gazed into the huge family room. On the wall above the shelves and storage for toys was a large flat screen that served as a calendar to outline the various activities of each member of the family for the next six weeks. Each person had a horizontal line. The weeks were broken into seven vertical days. This screen synced with her handheld tablet and contained all contact information, locations and names. All she had to do to find the details for one of the kids was tap the appropriate space on the screen and the information popped up.

The first row was dedicated to Edgar. Currently, the admiral was in DC, staying at the town house he'd owned for years.

Helena had taken the twins for a weeklong visit to her ex-husband in California. Afterward, she'd drop the kids off at a horseback riding camp on Catalina Island. She would then proceed to a movie set in Toronto for six weeks of filming.

The two littlest kids were at summer camp for eight weeks. Though the family could easily afford the finest camping experience available for the munchkins,

Prescott had convinced Helena that the kids could use a dose of reality in the woods. They were at a camp run by former SEALs where they would learn survival skills. *For four- and six-year-olds? Really?* The side bene-fit to this camp was that the entire staff were trained bodyguards. If there was danger, the little Prescotts were safe.

Thinking of safety reminded Lexie that being alone in a house that bad guys wanted to search might not be the smartest plan in the world. A shiver prickled her spine. She looked down at the coffee mug and saw that her hand was trembling. Ever since Helena had told her that her accident wasn't accidental, fear had been creeping around the edges of her consciousness. She kept looking over her shoulder. Remembered pain tensed her muscles.

Over and over, she told herself that there was noth-ing to worry about. This house had been searched by the CIA, the NSA and the admiral's assistant, Josh. They'd used an array of equipment designed to locate miniaturized circuits or magnets or whatever went into a flash drive. Josh had attempted to explain the technol-ogy before Stella grabbed the search probe and waved the long rod like a magic princess wand.

The thought of adorable blonde Stella brought a smile to Lexie's face. That was what she needed. Confidence and cool detachment were essential if she was going to figure out a way to use her special perspective to find the Damascus Cache. Mason might help. He'd be here by five o'clock, fewer than five hours. She could last until then.

The alarm on her watch went off, reminding her that she needed to make a phone call to check on the two oldest kids, who were staying with their mother in Seattle and taking a sailing trip on the Strait of Juan de Fuca. Taking her phone from the pocket of her jean shorts, she hit the speed dial for Meggie. The girl was far more likely to answer than Eddy Jr., who didn't like to be monitored.

The young woman's voice took on the chilly, whiny tone she used when adults were being annoying. She reported, "Our plane got in okay, but Mom's running late to pick us up. You'd almost think she wasn't thrilled to see us."

"Sarcasm?"

"What do you think?"

"More sarcasm."

"We only see her for an extended time twice a year. You'd think she'd make an effort. Oh, wait." Her voice lightened; she almost sounded happy. "Here she is. It's Mommy. 'Bye, Lexie."

"Have fun."

Her words were lost in Meggie's haste to get off the phone, and she wondered if Edgar had warned his former wife about the potential danger to the kids. Meggie was old enough to date, to be out on her own. The experts thought no one was in danger except for the admiral, but her experience had been different.

The image of her own car crash appeared in her mind. She mentally replayed those few seconds before impact. Could she have pumped the brakes or cranked the steering wheel harder? Had that bastard deliberately targeted her?

She didn't know. The perpetrators had never been identified, mostly because her dad had done what they wanted and quit the military. According to Helena, the car crash had nothing to do with the Damascus Cache. Nor was the anti-conspiracy group involved. The leader of AC-CD might have been using a different name at that time or she might even have been attacked by some other hater.

The attack was meant as a warning to men like her dad who dabbled in secrets. By hurting her, the bad guys were showing that their evil could reach all the way across the ocean and hurt loved ones in the States. She was a pawn to them. She meant nothing.

Yet that crash had changed her life and destroyed her future. In addition to the broken bones and torn muscles in her legs, the internal injuries were devastating. A collapsed lung, a punctured spleen and there had been nerve damage. She had required a hysterectomy.

The fragile dreams she'd had of a husband and family had been shattered. It wasn't fair for her to date or form a serious relationship. Maybe she should call Mason and tell him not to come. Clearly, he was a man looking for a settled-down relationship with the standard wife and kids. That was something she could never do.

A burst of rage spread from her belly to her chest. A flush crawled up her throat. Her cheeks flamed.

When she was taking care of the kids, she couldn't allow her emotions to get the better of her. She'd been holding back this outburst since Sunday. Now she was alone. So. Very. Alone.

She leaped from the stool onto the wood parquet floor. Her red sneakers thudded as she ran to the spacious entryway with its two-story ceiling and modern silver chandelier. A sweeping staircase going up led to the master suite and four other guest bedrooms, along with another suite for special guests. The kids had a wing of their own at the northern end of the house. Lexie slept there, but that wasn't where she was headed.

In the hallway beyond the foyer, she took the staircase to the lower level of the house. Tension kept building inside her. And the heat—she was on fire as she darted down a long hallway, passing storage spaces and the twenty-four-seat home theater. The southernmost room in the house was the home gym.

Too bad the swimming pool was empty! It would have been a relief to dive into the long narrow lap pool that stretched along the farthest edge of the room. The pool was surrounded on three sides by triple-pane bulletproof windows and had a fitted cover that matched the empty hot tub. With two young kids running around, the open water was too dangerous.

But the kids weren't here. Lexie was free to play rough. On the admiral's side of the gym were gray metal weights, a heavy punching bag, dumbbells, mats and a speed bag. Helena's side focused on movie-star exercises, like yoga and stretching. She had mirrors and a ballet barre and sometimes worked out to the music from Tchaikovsky's *Nutcracker* Suite. The admiral preferred Sousa marches played by the Marine Corps band.

Lexie took her cell phone from her pocket and placed it out of the way, then kicked off her sneakers and went through her karate warm-ups, starting by bouncing on the balls of her feet and progressing to stretches, squats and light kicks. Ever since she first started training with her brothers, she'd done this routine, and the repetition of familiar motions helped her get centered. Her tension wasn't gone; that would be far too simple. But she was beginning to loosen up. She added shouts to her kicks. "Ha. Ha. No fear. Ha."

She bounced over to the sound system. Amid the marches and the operas, there was a sound track of mixed selections that both the admiral and Helena liked. Lexie picked one. The first song: "Sweet Caroline." With the music cranked up loud, she sauntered toward the heavy punching bag suspended from the ceiling. With a fierce yell, she unleashed a series of kicks first with one leg, then the other. She expanded her attack to include a freestanding kick bag that popped back up when she knocked it down. She rolled down onto the mats and up again. Now she was singing along with the music. "Good times never seemed so good…"

Whirling and leaping and kicking, she made a circuit around the gym, practicing her poses—*Kihon Waza*—building her adrenaline, working off fear and dread. She came to a halt in front of Helena's wall of mirrors and stared at herself.

Under her freckles, her skin was flushed. She tore off her light sweatshirt. The T-shirt she wore underneath had sleeves too short to cover the puckered pink scar left by the bullet graze. She studied it. "What does one more matter?"

In the mirror, she had a full view of her legs. Her tan was marred by a faint patchwork of scars. The broken bones in her ankle had required surgery and both knees had had arthroscopic work done. More than once, she'd tried to tell herself that they were like tattoos. The difference was that she hadn't asked for these marks. It didn't matter that they weren't all that noticeable; she didn't want them.

"Those bastards," she muttered. How dare they come after her? She almost wished that her dad hadn't given in to them. If he'd kept up the fight, what would have happened to her? Would they have come after her in the hospital? After racing around the gym, she was pumped, energized, feeling no fear. She threw a couple of karate jabs and high kicks at her reflection in the mirror.

On the other side of the gym, she heard her cell phone ring. She dashed across and answered. It wasn't a number she recognized.

The voice on the other end of the call was patchy. "Are...surprise...ready."

"I can't hear you," she yelled. The loud background music didn't help. "Let me turn this down."

Quiet descended.

"There," Lexie said. "What did you say?"

"Are you alone?"

"What did you say?" Her breath froze in her lungs. "Who is this? What do you want?"

The call disconnected.

In spite of the static, she knew what he'd said. *Are you alone?* Anticipation of danger was often worse than the actual threat. She didn't scare easily. If somebody was coming for her, she would be prepared to take them on.

She peered through the wall of windows on the other side of the lap pool. Outside, there were trees and boulders, leafy bushes and shrubs. A stand of pine obscured the view down the slope to Henscratch Valley. When she saw movement, she jumped. A scrawny black squirrel darted across the top of a flat granite boulder.

Though certain that she'd locked the doors and set all the alarms, Lexie left the exercise room and went down the hallway to an unmarked door. Inside was a small room that the admiral called Command Central, which contained an impressive and extensive array of surveillance equipment. Monitors on sensors showed that none of the doors or windows had been opened or broken or compromised in any way. Outdoor cameras covered seven different angles. She studied each of these approaches to see if anything was out of place.

Nothing. She stared more closely. It all looked fine. That weird phone call was a fluke. Then she saw it. A rope dangled against the wall at the far north end of the house. Was it left over from a game the kids had been playing? *The roof?*

If an intruder intended to break into the house through the roof, he'd have to go through a window, which would set off an alarm. She'd heard nothing. The cameras didn't show anyone creeping through the surrounding forest. But there was that phone call…

She needed to go outside and take a look at the rope, and that meant she needed to be armed. Her karate skills were useful for surprise attacks, but she needed a gun for protection. She headed up the stairs to the main floor, where there was a locked gun cabinet.

In the front foyer, sunlight from high windows splashed against cream stucco walls and the gray tile floor. The overall style of the house was clean and modern with high ceilings and windows, so many windows. The branches of trees always seemed to be moving. Shadows changed and shifted.

Her ringtone sounded. She heard the breathiness in her voice. "Hello?"

"Are you alone?"

"Who is this?"

Chapter Ten

"If you're by yourself, I'll come to the front door." Mason heard the tension in her voice through the phone. "If somebody else is in the house, meet me by the garage."

"Come to the front," she said.

"I'll be there in five minutes."

When he'd gotten the call that morning from the admiral, hiring him to stay at the mansion in Aspen with Lexie for the next few weeks, Mason hadn't asked for much information. There was no need to question the best stroke of luck he'd had in years. He'd pounced on the chance to stay at a mansion in Aspen. Oh, and would he object if an attractive auburn-haired woman stayed with him? Mason couldn't say yes fast enough. He'd just won the lottery!

The edginess he'd heard in her voice gave him second thoughts...not enough to make him drop the assignment. No way would he back out. This job was fate, kismet, the way things were meant to be. Ever since he saw Lexie, he'd been thinking about her, trying to figure her out. The woman was a wealth of contradictions. She was optimistic and quick with a smile. But she was equally speedy with a karate kick to the groin and had done serious damage to that guy who attacked her outside the elevator. She was smart and had a degree in psychology. She kissed like an angel. But she had secrets—dark secrets—that gave her depth and complicated his job as a bodyguard.

He drove his Land Rover past a long building that had to be a garage designed to house a fleet of vehicles and ascended a sloping driveway toward a large structure with clean, bold architectural lines. It butted up to the granite hillside. Two stories in most places and three in others, the house was made of light cedar planks and accented with rectangular walls of concrete or natural stone. The angle of the entryway made him think of a boat, and the doorbell played a familiar sea chantey: "Yo ho ho, and a bottle of rum."

The door swung inward. Barefoot, Lexie dashed to the wall pad and punched in the code to deactivate the alarm. He noticed that she'd gathered a stockpile of weapons on the stairs: a rifle, two handguns and a hunting knife.

He glanced from the arsenal to her and back again. It was a little bit disconcerting. "Is there something I should know?"

"Never call a woman who might be alone and ask if she's alone."

"And why is that?"

"It's scary. You sound like a stalker." A smile played at the edges of her lips, but her dark eyes held a shimmer of real fear. "Or a pervert whose next question is going to be, 'And what are you wearing?' You should have explained."

"It was a bad connection."

"That's no excuse," she snapped. "Do I have to teach you phone manners? Like I do with the kids?"

I've been a naughty boy, nanny. Spank me. But she wasn't joking around. What had happened to the cute, funny, teasing Lexie? "You've made your point."

"Why did you want to know if I was alone?"

Her accusatory tone bugged him. Maybe he hadn't handled that phone call the right way, but it was time to let it go. She liked him, he knew it. Why else would she agree to a date? He pushed the door closed and dropped his backpack on the foyer floor. "The admiral suggested that—"

"The admiral? Why are you talking to him?"

"This morning he contacted TST Security and hired me for two weeks. It was his suggestion that I call ahead and see if you could meet me at the garage to open the door. I wanted to know if you were alone. If you were, I didn't want you running around outside."

"Why? Is there some kind of danger?"

Their earlier meetings had been natural, pleasant and encouraging. Now every word that came out of his mouth ticked her off. He didn't know how to approach her. If he told her to settle down or take a few deep breaths, she'd be insulted and then angrier. If he hid behind a fake smile and told her that there was nothing to worry about, she'd know he was lying.

There was only one approach that worked for him. "I'm going to tell you the truth."

She took a backward step. "Oh, my God, there is danger."

"I don't know," he said. "I need to do an assessment of the real and potential threat. That's what I always do when I come to a house as a bodyguard."

"You're guarding my body?"

Guarding wasn't the only thing he'd like to do to that slender, athletic body. He glanced at the scar from the bullet wound on her upper arm, which seemed to be healing well. Her snug coral T-shirt outlined her high, round breasts. Her cutoffs were frayed at the edges and short enough to display muscular legs with fading traces of scars that stood out against her tan.

It said something about her that she didn't try to hide the scars. Lexie was comfortable with who she was. Unapologetic and tough, she was the sort of woman he liked. She didn't take herself too seriously, as evidenced by the fact that each of her ten toenails was painted a different hue.

"I like your feet," he murmured.

"For a guy who wants to tell me the truth, you're very slow to say anything."

"Is there danger?" He repeated her question. "The admiral doesn't expect an attack on the house. Apparently they've done a lot of searching. Correct?"

She nodded and her curls bounced. "Mobs of technicians with special instruments have poked in every corner and crevice."

"So the house is clean. The Damascus Cache isn't here," he said. "But Prescott didn't want to take any chances in case the bad guys didn't get the word and tried to break in. It's better to be safe than sorry."

She pinned him with a gaze. "Did he say that?"

"As a matter of fact, those are his exact words."

"My dad says that all the time. Better to be safe, better to be safe, it's better to be safe than sorry."

The last time Mason saw her at the hotel, she'd had an issue with her dad being overprotective. Did that explain her current hostility? "Have you talked to him?"

"Not yet. It's kind of a big deal between us. I'm not sure whether I'm mad at him or whether I feel guilty or what…" Her voice trailed off. "You haven't heard the latest development between me and my dad, right?"

"I haven't."

She pivoted and marched down a hallway. "Do you want something cold to drink? We have soda, water, lemonade and beer."

Mason didn't follow obediently behind her like one of the Prescott kids. "You can't leave these weapons lying here."

"I'll clean up later."

Not good enough. He went to the staircase and picked up the rifle, handguns, ammo and knife. Even if no one else was in the house and the weapons weren't loaded, they needed to be returned to where they belonged. Taking a guess, he went down the hall behind the staircase. A light wood door stood open to his right, and he entered a very masculine office with an ornate, antique wood desk that looked as though it was seldom used for actual paperwork. The walls were lined with bookshelves. He spotted the gun cabinet behind the desk. The glass door stood unlocked and wide open. After he returned the guns to their places, he found the key in the middle desk drawer.

When he turned, he saw her leaning against the door frame with her arms folded below her breasts. She asked, "How did you know the key would be there?"

"It's the most logical place. Also the most obvious. I suggest hiding the key somewhere else. Better yet, put the gun cabinet in a room that isn't so easily accessible."

She exhaled in a huff. "You're right, of course. I've said the same thing to Prescott myself. With the kids getting into everything, we need to practice extreme gun safety."

"For now, I'll put the key back in the middle drawer. Tomorrow, we'll make adjustments."

"So you're going to be here two whole weeks."

He closed the middle drawer and came around the desk to stand before her. He was tired of her evasions. "Is that a problem?"

"Let's get you a drink."

When she turned, he grasped her uninjured arm above the elbow and held her gently but firmly. "Don't run away from me."

"I'm not." But she avoided looking at him.

It wasn't easy to protect anyone, much less a woman who was treating him like—what had she called him?— a stalker or a pervert. "If this is going to work, you have to trust me."

"It's not you, Mason. It's me."

"That's the oldest line in the book."

"Give me some time." Her gaze lifted, and he saw the pained vulnerability in her dark brown eyes. "I need to relax."

He released his hold. "Ten minutes."

"Fine."

This time, he followed her when she went down the hall and across the foyer to the kitchen. She still hadn't put on shoes. Her hips twitched in a way that was both athletic and sexy. Though she wasn't any taller than five feet three or four inches, her proportions were perfect and her legs were both slender and shapely.

In the kitchen she pointed to the stools at the counter. "Sit there. Now, what can I get you?"

"You mentioned lemonade."

She went to the side-by-side refrigerator, found the pitcher and poured a glass for each of them. She slid his across the marble-topped counter. It didn't escape his attention that she stayed on the opposite side rather than taking the stool next to him. She was keeping a distance between them.

He checked his wristwatch. He had promised ten minutes for her to relax. Only four minutes had passed, but he was too impatient to wait. "You said there was a development with your dad. I'd like to hear more."

"I have a question for you first."

When she took a sip of her lemonade, a bit of pulp stuck to her lip. She delicately removed it with the tip of her pink tongue…like a cat. An apt comparison, he thought. Like a cat, she captivated him with her graceful, clever moves. Like a cat, she turned her back without showing the least bit of interest in his response.

"Okay," she said. "You had arranged to pick me up for a date. But that's not why you're here right now. This is a job. Which is it?"

"A valid question." He translated her concern. "You want to know if it's unprofessional for me to agree to act as bodyguard for a woman I'm attracted to."

"Are you?" She brightened.

"Attracted?" He regretted the use of that word. "You're a good-looking woman. I'm a single man."

"And you're my bodyguard. If we're dating, isn't that a professional conflict?"

"I considered asking somebody else at TST to take this assignment." For about three and a half seconds, he'd considered. "It's not a problem. I can control my personal feelings. At five o'clock, I can quit being a bodyguard, and we'll have our date. Or not."

"How do you decide?"

"We'll know," he said. "Now it's my turn to ask you a question. Why did they leave you at the house alone?"

She pointed to a flat screen mounted on the wall in the room behind the kitchen. Unlike the rest of the sleek, stylish house, the family room had a more lived-in appearance. Toys were pulled off their shelves. A gang of stuffed animals sat side by side on the sofa facing the regular television. The blue and green colors with an occasional splash of yellow were cozy and welcoming.

He looked at the display on the flat screen. "A schedule?"

"It lists summer activities for all the kids and the admiral and Helena. There are camps and training programs. Helena will be filming in Canada. And the older kids are visiting their mom."

The closest Mason had ever come to a summer activity was when his brother, who was seven years older, took him camping in the mountains for a weekend with borrowed sleeping bags and beat-up cooking gear. The total cost for one of these weekends was almost nothing, but he had loved every moment. He wondered if these rich kids appreciated what they had. "Do the kids enjoy their activities?"

"Last summer, they seemed to like it a lot. Couldn't stop talking about it." Her gaze narrowed. She could see his attitude, his judgment. "You think the kids are overprivileged and spoiled."

"These kinds of activities are costly."

"I won't lie to you. It's a difficult balancing act to keep them grounded. The admiral makes sure that the older kids understand that they've received a lot and need to give back. They're involved in charity work."

Mason expected the admiral to raise responsible children. He also knew that it was easy for him to criticize someone else's child-rearing tactics when he didn't have kids of his own. Someday that would change, and he'd become a father. Someday soon, he hoped. He was ready for that challenge. "If everybody else is busy with activities, why do you need to stay at the house?"

"Two reasons. First, somebody needs to watch the house. Second, these schedules don't fit together seamlessly. I'm here to cover the downtime after one activity ends and the next begins. Sometimes Helena will fly in with some movie friends for an impromptu party.

Or her husband will hold a weekend conference with movers and shakers."

"But mostly you're at the house alone."

"Poor me," she said with a melodramatic rolling of the eyes. "Here I am…all alone in a multimillion-dollar mansion amid some of the most spectacular scenery in the world."

He tried to find something objectionable. "What about housework? Or special projects that the family wants you to do?"

"The maid service comes in once a week. If there's a special project, the housekeeper has already hired someone to do it. For cooking, all I need to do is make a phone call. The chef lives in town and is happy to come out and prepare a single meal or a whole regimen for any of Helena's crazy diets."

"Why doesn't the housekeeper live here in the summer?"

"The summer house-sitting used to be her job," she said. "But she's sixty years old and likes to travel. I wanted to do it, and the housekeeper gets much-deserved time off. She's taking two of her grandchildren to Australia for the month."

He looked down at his watch, and then held it so she could read the dial. "Time's up. You said that you needed ten minutes to relax before you could talk. Ready?"

Resolutely, she lifted her chin. "What do you want to know?"

"You're different." He could tell that she was scared,

but mentioning her fear seemed confrontational. "Something has changed from the last time I saw you."

"I learned that somebody tried to kill me." Her voice was eerily flat, as though she'd repeated those words a hundred times. "And they very nearly succeeded."

Chapter Eleven

When Mason showed up on the doorstep and said he'd been hired to be her bodyguard, Lexie had been relieved. The possibility of another attack had made her nervous. A deeper fear arose when Helena told her that the car crash hadn't been a random event. She'd been targeted. For the first time in her life, she'd felt like a victim.

Her life had been irreparably damaged. She'd never have kids. Every time she thought of that gaping hole in her life, she'd remember the black car with the tinted windows coming at her. Terror and rage would rise in her, again and again.

No way could she tell Mason about her hysterectomy. He was a family man, through and through. Solid, steady and stable, he was suited for a long-term relationship. That didn't work for her, but she was fairly sure that he'd be happy with a no-strings-attached affair. Most men were.

It wasn't her nature to have casual relationships, but her only other choice was to shove him out the door and insist on a less charming bodyguard. She didn't want to do that. She and Mason were most definitely attracted to each other. The moment he walked through the door, the air in the room had changed. The pheromones were flying. The snug fit of his jeans and the black T-shirt under his plaid shirt made her heart beat faster. Her fingers longed to embrace the breadth of his shoulders and slide down his muscular chest and abs. The timbre of his voice drew her closer.

He sat at the counter, sipping his lemonade and waiting for her to explain what she'd meant when she said that someone had tried to kill her. It was her turn to speak, and she knew it. But her throat had become a rusty hinge, holding back the words she needed to say.

"I'm not ready to talk about it," she creaked.

"Let's start with something easy," he said. "Why did you take out all those weapons?"

That, she could talk about. "I was in the gym when I got this creepy phone call."

"Ha-ha," he said.

"A really nasty voice," she teased, "ugly and evil. Then I went to Command Central, and I saw a rope dangling. I needed to check it out and didn't want to go in unarmed."

"You lost me. Let's go back to the gym."

"I'd love to."

"Can I see it? The admiral sent me blueprints of the security system and the house. The gym is huge, and I know Prescott would have the best equipment."

"Let's go. This way." She led to the staircase leading down. "I need to get my shoes, anyway."

Mason was a big man, several inches over six feet, but his hiking boots hardly made a sound when he walked across the wood parquet floor. Silence accompanied his movements. Not stealth. He had nothing to hide. But there was a stillness that came from his sheer, unshakable confidence.

At the foot of the stairs, he made a detour, turning right and opening the door to Command Central. Apparently, he already knew his way around the house. As he stood in the doorway, his gaze flicked from screen to screen, taking in all the dials and knobs. Again, he seemed to know how everything worked without having her explain. Why shouldn't he? Security was his job, after all.

"Show me where you saw this dangling rope."

Taking a seat at one of the consoles, she flipped though several views from cameras outside the house. She paused and pointed. "There it is. That's the north end of the house near the kids' bedrooms."

"It goes up to the roof," he said.

"But there haven't been any break-ins. If any of the windows or openings onto the roof were tampered with, an alarm would go off."

"I'm familiar with this system." He leaned over her shoulder to tap the keyboard, and the warmth of his body wrapped around her. His citrus and nutmeg aftershave teased her nostrils.

"What are you doing?" *Other than smelling good and driving me crazy.* "The screen went dark."

"I'm doing a rewind," he said. "I programmed it to go backward in twelve-hour jumps. Good eye, by the way. I never would have noticed the rope."

A picture on the screen came back into focus. The

shadows and light were different, but nothing else had changed. The rope still dangled.

There was another picture and another and another. He leaned even closer. His cheek was even with hers. If she swiveled her head, she'd be looking directly into his ear.

He pointed to a time stamp in the corner of the screen. "This is Tuesday morning."

The next picture filled the screen. Together, they said, "No rope."

Using the keyboard, Mason had both arms around her, though the low back of the office chair separated them. It would have made sense for her to move, but he hadn't suggested it, and she liked being nestled in his arms. He played forward on the screen until he found Tuesday at four o'clock. The long shadow from the house almost obscured the appearance of a man dressed in jeans and a black Windbreaker. He wore a cap with the visor pulled down. His features were hidden.

Mason put the image on pause while he juggled dials to improve the resolution on the screen. "His jacket says CIA across the back."

"Tuesday was when Agent Collier and his men from the CIA were at the house, searching for the Damascus Cache. This guy could have been any one of them."

"To your knowledge, were they outside the house?"

"No, but I wasn't keeping track of what they were doing. You need to talk to Collier for verification."

As she watched the intruder, her muscles began to tense. The dangling rope indicated that someone had been there, but she was hoping for an innocent explanation. The intruder had a hook attached to the rope. He tossed it onto the roof three times before it caught. Then he used the rope to scale the wall.

"He's fast," Mason said. "That didn't even take five minutes."

"And we still haven't gotten a clear look at his face."

Mason straightened and stepped back from the console. His demeanor had changed; he'd gone from light to dark. "Do you want to know the worst thing about a risk assessment?"

"I think I know," she said. "Sometimes you find danger."

He nodded, then hit a button to pause the playback on the screen. "I'd like to see the gym before we finish the assessment."

She padded barefoot down the hall to the keypad outside the gym. "The code is B-U-N-S and never changes. We have the room locked to keep little Todd and Stella away from the heavy equipment."

He trooped inside behind her. Helena's Pilates equipment, mirror and ballet barre were of little interest to him. His eyes lit up when he saw the array of weights and punching bags.

"Beautiful," he murmured with undisguised lust. He rubbed his palm across his close-cropped blond hair and turned toward the sunlit forest outside the wall of windows. He inhaled a deep breath, and his muscular chest expanded inside the black T-shirt. A wide smile stretched across his face.

It would have felt good to have him look at her with such naked longing. She huffed. "Do you love it?"

"I could live here."

"A gym rat, I knew it."

"I haven't always been that way." Bouncing on the balls of his feet, he went to the speed bag and punched it a couple of times with his bare knuckles. "When my brother was killed, I needed something to get rid of the tension, know what I mean?"

She did, indeed. Lexie relied on her karate exercises to relieve stress. She crossed the gym to the more feminine side and slipped into her red sneakers.

He shucked off his plaid shirt, picked up a ten-pound dumbbell and did a few curls. "I used to exercise until I could barely stand up. I'd stagger home, fall into the sack and my eyes would pop open. Couldn't sleep. My brain wouldn't shut down. I kept thinking that Matt wasn't really dead. It must be a case of mistaken identity. I couldn't let him go… Still can't."

She'd been so caught up in the tragedies of her life that she'd forgotten about him. When the SecNav had commended his brother's heroic action, she'd seen the pained and haunted look on Mason's face. A Purple Heart was a great honor, but he'd rather have his brother back.

Not that Mason was the type to indulge in a pity party. Automatically, he transferred the weight to his other hand to balance the exercise as he strolled toward the covered lap pool and hot tub. "Do you ever use these?"

"Yes for the tub. Not often for the pool. It takes

thousands of gallons of water to fill and when the little ones are around, it's not safe." She wasn't ready to drop the subject of his brother. "How old were you when he died?"

"He was killed," Mason said. "Saying he died implies that there was something natural about it. Murder is an unnatural act. Six years ago, he was murdered in Afghanistan. I was finishing up college, deciding if I should go for my master's."

She hadn't pictured him as a college student. "What was your major?"

"International studies." He continued to pump the dumbbell as he walked the perimeter of the long lap pool. "Back then, I was young and innocent and thought I could make sense of the world. I learned that no single country can take credit for being the worst mess. They're all bad, even us."

"I could've figured that out." She wanted to know more about him, more details. "How did you get into security?"

Standing in front of her, he stopped pacing and dug into his jeans pocket. In his hand, he held a key chain. The brass fob was a four-leaf clover with TST Security written in a half circle across the top. Three of the leaves were a lucky-Irish green. One was red.

"I don't remember who came up with the idea," Mason said. "Me and Matt were buddies with Sean and Dylan, and we thought we'd be outstanding crime fighters. Just before Matt was killed, we sat down and talked about the possibilities. Sean's the oldest, and he had done a stint in the FBI. Dylan is a computer whiz, which is necessary for security work. Matt had top-notch military training. And I was a political wonk who could get by in seven languages."

"Seven? I'm impressed."

"Don't be. With language, you've got to use it or lose it, and I haven't kept it up. I turned into a gym rat. Now I'm the muscle in the group."

He was so much more than muscle. Not that she had any complaints about his body. But she found herself being drawn to his mind and the unique way he saw the world. For sure, he was cynical. But there was a redeeming ray of hope that kept him from being bitter.

With her forefinger, she pointed to the three green leaves. "These stand for you, Sean and Dylan."

He raised the red leaf to his lips and kissed it. "This stands for Matt. He's always watching over us."

If he was trying to seduce her, he was sticking to an extremely low-key approach. And yet she wanted him. She wanted him desperately. Maybe because she hadn't been dating much for the past year and a half, Lexie was ready to pounce, to drag him off to her bedroom and get sexy. Better yet, they could strip down right here in front of the mirror. Practically panting, she asked, "What comes next?"

"I'm not finished with my risk assessment."

Inwardly, she groaned.

He continued, "The dangling rope indicates that somebody might have tried to break in. But I need to talk to Agent Collier and find out if he sent one of his men up onto the roof."

"Then what?"

"I should familiarize myself with the house and make sure all security functions are working properly."

Following someone around and watching while he did his job wasn't her idea of a great time. Besides, she seriously doubted that she'd be able to trail him all the way around the massive house without tearing off his clothes. "I'll leave you to your work."

As she went down the hall toward the staircase, she heard him call after her, "We have a date at five."

"How should I dress?"

"You decide."

She had a few ideas for her outfit. Maybe she'd go casually seductive with shorts and a bare midriff. She had a fancier outfit with a plunging neckline. Maybe she should go for a wraparound dress that could be removed with one light tug on the sash. Or she might decide to wear nothing at all.

Chapter Twelve

While he was exploring the main floor of the house, Mason's call to Agent Collier finally went through. He went into the formal office with the locked gun cabinet and sat at the massive, carved desk. Being in a classy office/library like this made him feel like a high-ranking officer. Tilting back in the swivel chair, he stretched out his legs and rested the heels of his hiking boots on the desk blotter.

"I'm at Admiral Prescott's house," Mason said. "Lexie told me that you and your men were here on Tuesday."

"Yes, I brought four agents." Collier's accent sounded thicker over the phone. "We discovered evidence that we weren't the first to go through the house."

"What did you find?"

"An infestation of bugs." He chuckled at his pun. "There were twelve listening devices planted throughout the house. Also, we found three cameras that weren't part of the Prescott security system."

The blueprints showed three cameras inside the house: one in the hallway outside the children's bedrooms, one in the kitchen where there were French doors and one in the lobby. "Are there more than three cameras inside the house?"

"That is all," he said. "While we were there, we made a thorough search, except for one room."

"Which room? And why not?"

"In the lower level, there is a safe room with a combination lock and a key. According to the magnificent Helena Christie Prescott, her husband possesses the only key. He was still at the Pentagon."

Keeping it locked was counterintuitive. A safe room was supposed to be entered easily by the people who lived in the house. Once they were safely locked inside away from any threat, the room should be impregnable to outsiders.

He jolted forward to sit upright in the chair and spread the blueprints for the house across the desktop. "I'm assuming they don't actually use that room as it was intended. Is it storage?"

"Helena says yes." Collier mumbled a few words that might have been curses. "Extreme valuables are kept there—artworks, statues, antiques."

"What about deeds and paperwork?" The safe room seemed like the ideal place to hide the Damascus Cache. The admiral was from an older generation where papers and documentation were all carefully stored in locked boxes in banks or in safes.

"Helena would not say more. But I suspect she has a key. Among the valuables, there must have been jewelry. *Her* jewelry."

"She stonewalled you."

"It was disturbing," Collier said, "to come all the

way to Aspen only to be denied full access to the premises."

"It's not a bad trip."

"Marvelous scenery," he agreed, "and the gym is among the best home facilities I have ever seen."

Tracing with his forefinger, Mason found the safe room on the blueprint. It was located on the lower level at the opposite end of the hallway from the gym. The house butted up against a cliff with one floor stacked on top of another. At the northern end, the safe room would be underground. The level on top of it was the wing with the children's bedrooms, where the rope had been left dangling. Mason wondered if there was any connection.

"In your search," he said, "did any of your men go outside?"

"No, nor did we search the outbuildings, including the horse barn or the garage or anywhere that an outsider could approach without help from someone inside the house. We operated under the theory that the AC-CD believed the admiral had hidden the cache, and it was probably smaller than a matchbox—the size of a computer flash drive."

"Can you think of a reason why anyone wearing a CIA Windbreaker would want access to the roof?"

There was a moment's silence. In a moment like this, Mason wished he had Sean's training with the FBI. Sean had studied criminal psychology and profiling; he knew the various techniques of questioning. Sean would have known if Agent Collier's moment of hesitation had any significance. It seemed logical that he was hiding something. Was it guilt? Was Collier after the cache for his own nefarious purposes? Or was he embarrassed about his men breaking protocol?

"I require an explanation," Collier finally said. "Why do you think my men were on the roof?"

"One man." Mason leaned forward, resting his elbows on the desk. He wished he could see Collier. It was easier to catch someone in a lie when you were face-to-face with the liar. "An outdoor surveillance camera shows a man in a CIA Windbreaker throwing a grappling hook onto the roof and climbing up a rope attached to the hook."

"Not one of my men. Did the camera show this man coming down?"

"I haven't bothered to look," Mason admitted. "None of the alarms for the windows or the rooftop openings were activated."

"Of course they weren't. We shut them down."

"What? You turned off the security system?"

"Not all day. Occasionally." His voice was faster, his accent heavier. "We accidentally set it off twice. Then we made the decision to turn it off when we were searching."

Panic shot through Mason. He surged to his feet so quickly that his head whirled. How could he have been so careless? He should have known that the CIA would turn the system off. The intruder might have entered the house through the attic. *He might still be here.* "I've got to go. Thanks, Collier."

He dashed out of the office, down the hall and into the foyer. Lexie's bedroom was somewhere on the sec-

ond floor, north end, but he didn't know which one was
hers. He flew up the staircase, taking the steps two at
a time. The landing stretched into a balcony that over-
looked the foyer. Leaded glass windows above the front
door admitted a splash of natural sunlight.

He called her name. "Lexie, are you here? Lexie?"

Skylights overhead kept the long hallway from being
too dark, but he flicked a switch that lit sconces along
the wall. Afternoon light poured through the window
at the end of the hall, which was where they'd spotted
the rope dangling.

His fingers drew into fists. He wasn't sharp enough
to handle this job. Sean's deductive skills would have
been more useful. Or Dylan's cleverness with computers. If anything happened to Lexie because of him,
Mason would never forgive himself.

"Lexie?" Where was she? Did she step outside for
a walk? She would have told him, wouldn't she? He
should have laid down ground rules. "Lexie?"

He took out his phone and punched in her number.
It rang six times and went to voice mail. He charged
down the hall and back again. Maybe she'd gone to
the gym.

He hit redial for her phone. As he stalked down
the hallway, he heard her ringtone, a song from *Mary
Poppins*. The cheerful, perky music was coming from
inside a room. He paused outside the first door to the
right of the staircase and listened. "Just a spoonful of
sugar..."

"Lexie!"

Without waiting for her to answer, he shoved open

the door. She was nowhere in sight. Her phone in the center of the bed gave a final chirp and went quiet. The little red sneakers she'd been wearing peeked out from the edge of her comforter beside her neatly made bed. Her room was a good size, with a large window and a view of distant snow-capped peaks.

Where was she? He wanted to tear apart the bed and fling open the closet door. Then he heard the rumble of the shower from the adjoining bathroom. In a whoosh, he exhaled the tense breath he'd been holding. *She's fine. In the shower. Perfectly fine.* The classy thing for him to do would be to exit, close the door and knock on it until she answered.

Shower steam rushed from the bathroom door when she opened it a crack and poked her head through. "Mason? What's up?"

He strode across her bedroom. Without saying a word, he pulled her close against his chest and nuzzled her wet hair.

"Is something wrong?" She wriggled in his grasp.

"It's okay now." He held her closer. Obviously, he owed her an explanation, but all he wanted right now was to feel her energy and know that she hadn't been hurt. There was nothing between them but a bath towel, and his behavior was totally inappropriate. He didn't care.

Her arms wrapped around his torso and her wiggling subsided as she settled into a comfortable stance. In spite of the twelve-inch difference in their heights, their bodies fit together nicely. Her soft curves molded to his hard edges.

After a final squeeze, he took a step back. She managed to grab her towel before it fell, but not quickly enough that he didn't catch a glimpse of her left breast and the dusky rose of her nipple. As wardrobe malfunctions went, this was modest.

Still, she blushed. "Have you lost your mind?"

If he stood here and tried to make sense of his tension, panic and guilt for having failed her and failed at his job, Mason was fairly sure that he'd dissolve into an incoherent, babbling mess. All he could do was stare at the towel and wish for it to be gone.

"In the hall," he managed to choke out. "You get dressed. I'll be in the hall."

He made a crisp pivot and went out the door. In the long hallway, he was unable to make himself stand still. He paced up and down, trying to burn off the emotional shock he'd felt when he realized that the intruder could still be in the house. Though it was extremely unlikely, he and Lexie had to go downstairs to Command Central and play through the tape until they found him climbing down. Mason cursed himself. Why hadn't he done that in the first place? *What goes up must come down.* It was child's play to recall that simple formula.

Sean would have told him that you should never trust the security system. People relied too much on electronics. On the other hand, Dylan would have put his faith in the computerized security and pointed out that if it weren't for the outdoor surveillance camera, they wouldn't have seen anything.

Lexie joined him in the hall. She had on her cutoffs and a fresh T-shirt with hummingbirds on the front. She'd stuck her feet into flip-flops that displayed her multicolored toenails. Her damp hair was tucked behind her ears. She smelled like a garden of lilies, lilacs, roses and honeyed flowers.

She cleared her throat. "The last thing I remember you saying is that you were going to call the CIA."

"Agent Collier was helpful." He gestured for her to come with him as he descended the grand staircase into the foyer and the less grand set of stairs into the lower level. "Collier didn't send any of his men onto the roof, so our intruder must have swiped a Windbreaker so he could walk around unnoticed. A simple disguise."

"Or not," she said. "One of his agents could be a traitor."

"Correct." He liked that she was smart and saw all the possibilities. "The worst part is that Collier had the security turned off at various times during the day while he was searching. We never saw the man on the roof climb down."

"And you thought he might have gotten into the house?" Her tone was incredulous. "That he was hiding out in the attic?"

"It's possible."

"Since the weekend, there have been more than thirty people coming into and going out of this house. Managing to hide out from that mob would take some fancy footwork."

"Humor me, okay? Let's just see if he left."

They were in Command Central. He sat in front of the screen where they had watched the intruder climbing onto the roof. As Mason started running the images in fast-forward, she peeked over his shoulder, bringing that delightful fragrance with her. He inhaled deeply, trying to identify all the scents. The rose was from a soap from a hotel he knew in Grand Junction. Lilies and lilacs—the purple tones—were from a shampoo a former girlfriend had used. The honey sweetness emanated from Lexie herself. "Honey," he murmured.

"What?"

"You smell like honey."

"Honeysuckle," she corrected. "It's the fragrance of a moisturizing cream I use on my arms and legs. Is it too strong?"

"I like it."

"Colorado is the worst for dryness. I'm always smearing on moisturizer and guzzling water."

Whatever beauty regime she was using, it worked. Fresh from the shower, her clean skin glistened. The freckles across her cheeks were more obvious than those on her tanned arms and legs. She hadn't hidden any of those polka dots under layers of makeup.

"There." She pointed to the screen. "The guy in the CIA jacket is climbing down the rope."

Mason verified the time stamps on the footage and mentally calculated. "Our intruder was on the roof for less than an hour. We should go up there and see what he was doing."

"Do you need me to help you?"

To help him? Not really. But he wanted her to be with him until he was one hundred percent certain that the house was secure. "You're coming with me."

With her fists on hips and her legs slightly akimbo, she planted her feet as though taking a stand. "You want my help, right?"

"Sure." He didn't want to argue. When he'd thought she might be in danger, he used up his adrenaline spurt of panic tracking her down to the shower. His current energy level was more laid-back, less intense. "I'm not letting you out of my sight until I'm certain that it's safe."

"That's not fair. I'm—"

"Coming with me," he said, finishing her sentence. "What's the fastest, easiest way to get to where the rope is dangling?"

Her slender shoulders twitched in a shrug. She went to the door and turned left. "This way."

She marched down the hallway in the lower level toward the north end of the house. He could track their depth by the shape of the windows. At the southern point of the lower level—the gym—the windows were floor to ceiling. Heading toward the staircase, the windows were garden level. Then they were near the ceiling. In the last forty feet, there were no windows at all.

"We're underground," he said. "Is the safe room down here?"

"How did you know about the safe room?"

"I have blueprints," he reminded her.

The hallway ended in a T-shape. To his right was an

open archway leading to what appeared to be storage. Lexie went past him and closed it. "This isn't supposed to be open. Not a good place for the little ones to play."

The door directly in front of him was matte black and mounted in a metal frame. There was a dial on the front and a door handle. "Have you ever been inside there?"

"When I first took the nanny job, Helena showed me how to get inside. It's really safe but scary. Going in there is a last resort."

"They don't call it a panic room for nothing."

"The Prescotts use it as a safe for their important papers, the furs, jewelry and a couple of paintings and sculptures." Her eyes darted nervously. "You know, stuff like that."

Lexie's furtive behavior made him think she was hiding something. Maybe the artworks hadn't been purchased legitimately. If so, it made sense that Helena didn't want Agent Collier and his men poking around in there. "Can you show me how to open it?"

She eyed him suspiciously. "Planning to steal a mink and a tiara?"

"I was thinking it might be useful to have a safe room. In case the bad guys show up."

She reached over and twirled the dial on the front of the door. "The entry code is different from the rest of the house, and it resets after every time it's opened. I can track the number down by accessing household computer files."

Access to the panic room was meant to discourage anyone from going inside. If there had been any reason to suspect Helena of hiding the Damascus Cache, Mason would look in this room first.

At the left end of the T-shape at the end of the hall, she punched numbers into a keypad and opened the door. She skipped up a flight of stairs, and he followed. They were in the forest.

Sunlight dappled the leaves of chokecherry shrubs and grasses while the breeze whispered through the high branches of surrounding pines. He loved being in the mountains. The air tasted fresher here. The light was clearer.

He hiked up the slope to where the rope was dangling. Though it was only a one-story climb to the roof, Mason stayed below Lexie. If she slipped, he'd catch her. Using the rope, she ascended quickly.

Standing on the rooftop, she spread her arms to take in the wide vista. "Great view. The admiral is thinking about putting in solar panels."

Far below the high cliff where the house perched, the relatively flat land of Henscratch Valley stretched to another jagged ridge. A small herd of cattle grazed. A hawk swooped across clear blue skies. He inhaled and exhaled slowly. This was a king of the world moment. He was overwhelmed by the spacious grandeur and would have preferred sitting and soaking in all this natural beauty.

But he had a job to do. His footing on the thermal asphalt shingles felt solid. The landscape of the roof was slants, slopes, gables and skylights, which Lexie scrambled over like a mountain goat in flip-flops.

Mason concentrated on figuring out why the intruder had climbed up here. As far as he could tell, the wiring on the windows hadn't been tampered with. The alarm system appeared to be intact.

About halfway down the north wing—an area that was directly above the children's bedrooms—he noticed a small but potentially lethal device tucked against the edge of a skylight.

It was a bomb.

FROM HIS PERCH fifteen feet off the ground, Tony dropped his binoculars into his lap and leaned back against the thick trunk of the tall pine tree he'd chosen for his surveillance point when he followed them outside. While they were in the house, he was able to keep track of them using a heat-sensing infrared camera that showed their images in red outlined against the cooler green of their surroundings. He'd been watching when Lexie and the bodyguard went in different directions…and when they came together for a steaming-hot embrace.

Tony almost felt sorry for the guy. He was falling for Lexie, which meant she'd wait until she had him wrapped around her little finger, and then she'd dump him. That was what she did. He wasn't the only guy in Texas to get booted from his relationship by little Miss Francine Alexandra.

On the rooftop, she scooted toward the escape rope. The bodyguard warned her to get away; he'd located one of the tiny, cell-phone-activated bombs Tony had planted.

This guy didn't know much about explosives. These

bomb charges weren't big enough to do serious damage. They were meant to be used as a distraction.

Tony wasn't going to blow up the house. Directives from the leader were clear: no one was to be harmed, especially not the kids. *And isn't that too bad?* Tony would have enjoyed inflicting harm on those spoiled brats, enough harm that they'd understand that they couldn't have everything they wanted. Sometimes your mama promises a kiss but you get a slap in the face.

He'd leave a few scars behind to remind them…like the scars on Lexie's legs.

Life wasn't all sunshine and butterflies. Why was the leader protecting these people, treating them as if they were special? Tony was sick and tired of pussy-footing around.

Being cautious wasn't getting the job done. If they didn't get their hands on the Damascus Cache soon, they'd miss out on a big payday. And there were other ways than kidnapping the admiral and trying to get him to talk. Tony had presented an idea about using Lexie as a hostage to leverage the admiral into giving up the cache.

Getting his hands on her would be easy. All he had to do was get that damn bodyguard out of the way. He closed his eyes and imagined Lexie all trussed up, naked and helpless. He'd take his time getting to know her body again, seeing her quiver when he squeezed her soft breasts, hearing her moan when he traced the folds between her legs. She'd cry when he slapped her face. She'd fall to her knees and beg for his mercy.

Tony was tempted to put his plan to kidnap Lexie into effect. The leader could deal with the consequences. That would be his problem.

Chapter Thirteen

The Aspen fire department had done such an excellent job that Lexie wished the kids were home to watch. Less than twenty minutes after she'd called in to report the bomb, the shiny red truck pulled up to the front door with sirens blaring. Fortunately, she and Mason had been standing by to open the door, because the local firemen and one woman were armed with axes and ready to hack their way through to the nonexistent flames.

Their search of the roof had been eventful. They found six small cell-phone-activated charges, none of which would result in a major explosion. "More like fireworks than a bomb" was how the chief explained the devices. "More like a bomblet." But those nasty little bomblets were a fire danger and needed to be removed.

The fire department crew had used a long, basket-like tool to scoop up the bomblets and then deposit them in a shiny metal sphere called a blast chamber. This marked the first time they'd used the blast chamber.

When all the devices had been collected and the chamber had been locked up tight, the threat was contained.

The crew seemed happy to have a new piece of equipment to play with. They were cheerfully discussing procedure for setting off the explosives when the chief pulled Lexie to one side and gave her a report sheet to fill in and sign. Out of respect for the admiral, he wouldn't conduct a formal investigation, but he would appreciate being kept in the loop. He was concerned because of the attack at the hotel, but the fire chief didn't have a beef about jurisdiction. He'd rather not be in charge.

Before he and the crew drove away in their shiny red truck, he'd consulted with Mason. As she watched the two men, Lexie realized that her bodyguard hadn't changed from the clothes he wore when he arrived, minus the plaid shirt. Not that there was anything wrong with the way he was dressed. She liked the simple, masculine look of his black T-shirt and jeans and hiking boots. But was it date appropriate?

The sun slipped lower in the sky, and Lexie checked her phone for the time. It was 4:35 p.m. Mason hadn't mentioned their date. Nor had she.

It seemed that the idea had simply faded away. Why bother dating when they had a mansion to themselves? If they wanted, they could fill the hot tub or watch a movie in the downstairs theater or make themselves a gourmet dinner. There was no need to go out, and he hadn't said a word about where they'd be going. She exhaled a disappointed sigh. It wasn't important.

She entered the house, climbed the staircase and

went to her bedroom, where she sprawled facedown on the queen-size bed with the pale blue striped comforter. Lazily, she dragged her fingers through her shoulder-length hair that had dried in messy tangles. She should have done a quick blow-dry, but Mason had been in such a frantic hurry when he pulled her from the shower. He'd been afraid that something bad had happened to her. In his eyes, she had seen the glimmer of real fear.

In spite of the muscles, he had a sensitive streak. If he needed to kick ass, he could. But he was smart—smart enough to know that not all problems could be solved with his fists or by running away. Mason didn't fit the stereotype of a muscle head with a great bod and no brain. That was as unfair as the myth of the dumb blonde or the fiery redhead.

There was a rap on her door.

She sat up on the bed. "Come in."

Smoothly, Mason stepped into the room and closed the door. "I wanted to let you know that I'm going to be a few minutes late for our date."

"Is it still on?"

"I didn't cancel."

"If you don't want to go out, we don't have to bother."

"Not a bother." He crossed the room and lowered himself on the bed beside her. "It's my pleasure."

"Why?"

And why was she looking this gift horse in the mouth? If a man wanted to be nice to her, she ought to let him. She was always quick to throw up her defenses, maybe too quick.

"I like you," he said. "Dating is what happens when a man likes a woman. It's a great American ritual. Part of our culture."

"Our culture?" That description seemed a bit too grand. "You might be overstating."

"As an international studies major, I'd argue that American dating habits are one of our biggest exports. Going out with one boy, one girl and one car—it's the American style. No chaperones. No arranged courtships. And we definitely don't require dowries or bride tokens."

"What's a token?"

"A payment I'd make to your father for your hand. You know, a golden goblet and six goats."

"Only six?"

"You're sort of skinny."

"You pig." She smacked him on the arm. His easy conversation was relaxing her. The defenses were falling. "It's terrible that families used to do that to their women, selling them off for livestock. It shows no respect."

"Or is it the other way around? Their daughters are so precious that they demand payment for them."

"If it was acceptable, my dad would be like that. He'd ask such a ridiculously high price that nobody could pay it, and I'd never leave home."

"Did you get a chance this week to talk to him?"

"Not really." She collapsed backward on the bed. She'd talked to her dad but hadn't told him everything. She hadn't confronted him about the crash, about how it was his damned fault. It didn't seem that there was anything positive to be gained from that confrontation.

Mason stretched out beside her on the bed. Lying side by side should have felt intimate, but she was doing her best not to put him in that category. She wanted Mason to be a friend, someone she might know two years from now. Not a boyfriend. Her lovers came and went as fast as a revolving door.

"Did you tell him everything?" he asked.

"What do you mean?" Had Helena blabbed to him, too? "What do you know?"

"Only what you've told me," he said. "He was treating you like a child, saying that you had to come home at the first sign of danger."

"Right." Now she understood why her dad had been so concerned about her safety. "I kept a few things to myself."

"Like what?"

"He's so anxious to interfere in my life now, but there was a time when he should have protected me but didn't."

"That doesn't sound like a marine."

Though her bed was queen-size, the space seemed to shrink around them until it was as small as a camping cot. If she and Mason were going to have any sort of relationship, she needed to trust him and tell him the whole story. She scooted around until she was sitting cross-legged beside him, looking down at his handsome face.

There was something she'd wanted to do from the first time she saw him, and now seemed like the right time. She reached out and rubbed her palm back and forth over his buzz cut. His short, razor-cut blond hair tickled.

He caught hold of her wrist. "Is there a reason you're petting my head like a dog?"

The bristly haircut actually did remind her of a sleek-coated dog, like a Great Dane. "I wanted to see how the buzz felt."

"This is your one and only warning. If you treat me like a dog again, I will get you good." He released her wrist and lay back on the bed, staring up at the ceiling. "This thing with your dad, did it happen a long time ago?"

"It was the car crash when I was twenty. I told you about it." His teasing kept her from sinking into depression when she talked about the worst trauma of her life. "I always thought it was an accident, even though they never found the guy who ran into me. A hit-and-run accident. And I was lucky that another driver came along to help me and to call for assistance."

She shook away the dark, terrifying images. She'd seen the car coming at her. Through the dark-tinted glass, she couldn't make out the features of the driver.

Mason's large hand rested on her knee. Again, he wasn't trying to be sexy. His touch was meant to soothe her and offer comfort. When she gazed into his blue eyes, they seemed to absorb and reflect her pain at the same time.

"The driver," she said without a tremble, "was sent by enemies of my father. He attacked me as a warning for my dad, a warning for the whole CIA, MI6 secret-agent community. They struck at me. I paid the price for all the other families."

"Finally," he whispered.

"Finally what?" she snapped irritably. "What are you talking about?"

"One of the first things you said to me was someone tried to kill you and very nearly did. Then you made a hundred and one excuses not to tell me. Now you trust me enough to tell me."

"Maybe I trust you. Maybe a little."

"Did your father know that you were the intended target of a hit?"

"No." At least, she didn't think so. "He couldn't have known. If he had, my brothers would be protecting me."

"When he was informed, what did your dad do?"

"The bad guys wanted him to quit the exercise he was involved with. He did. Then he took early retirement, left the marines and came home to take care of me."

So many emotions swirled inside her that she couldn't tell her anger from her fear from her guilt. Had she ruined her father's life, causing him to leave the work he loved? Or had he ruined hers by placing her in the line of fire?

"We never talked about it," she said. "He doesn't know that I know about the terrorist and how he quit to protect me."

Mason sat up on the bed. Gently, he stroked her hair off her cheek and tucked it behind her ear. "It's not your fault that your father chose to leave the marines and put you first. And it's not his fault that you were in the crash."

"Then who do I blame?"

"The hit-and-run driver. He's the one who directly hurt you. But you could also blame the larger organization that sent him. Blame the war. Blame the ongoing struggles. Blame humanity."

"It's not fair."

"And there's nothing you can do to change it. It's in the past."

With a frustrated little sigh, she leaned into him and rested her cheek against his broad chest. Holding her, he slid back into a reclining position. They were crosswise on the bed with one of his legs halfway off and his foot on the floor. She snuggled into the nook below his chin, rubbing her cheek against his soft T-shirt.

"I want the past to be different," she said.

"Good luck with that."

She wanted to be whole and complete. If he wanted children, she wasn't the right woman for him. *Keep your distance, Lexie.* It was smarter to end this relationship right now, before she got too wrapped up in him, before he became a part of her and dumping him was as painful as tearing off a limb.

She disentangled away from his embrace and got off the bed. Straightening her shoulders, she asked, "What should I wear for our date?"

LEXIE WAS GLAD she'd paid no attention to his suggestion of an outfit with a very short skirt and a casual but very low-cut top. Her choice for their date was skinny jeans with cowgirl boots and a turquoise blouse under a short, lightweight leather jacket. She'd be warm and comfy and looked pretty good with her hair held back by a thin gold band.

Mason had showered but hadn't shaved. The stubble on his chin was darker than the hair on his head and made him look a full five years older. Adding five years balanced out his youthful buzz cut, which made him look younger. She had calculated his age at twenty-seven or twenty-eight, which was a good match for her at twenty-five. On the drive to the restaurant in the hills outside Aspen, she'd been studying his profile. He had a classic Roman nose, but otherwise his features were Scandinavian, like a Viking's.

It was half past six when he pulled out her chair and tucked her into her seat at the table. After his lecture about the proper rituals of dating, he'd better be sharp about performing all those jacket-holding, door-opening jobs. No surprise, he was skilled at acting the role of a gentleman, which made her feel so ladylike that she crooked her pinkie when she lifted her water goblet, took a sip and looked at him over the rim.

"Did you ever complete your risk assessment of the house?" she asked.

"If I hadn't completed it, we wouldn't be here. In spite of the bomblets on the roof, the security system is intact and effective. Between the electronic surveillance, the alarms and Command Central, nobody is getting into that house without announcing their presence. The admiral told me his system was state of the art, and he didn't lie."

"Which makes me wonder." She set down her glass and smoothed the linen tablecloth. Since this was a nice dining establishment that was geared toward adults, not children, she hadn't been here. "If he's not really worried about security, why hire you?"

"Ever heard the phrase 'CYA'?"

"Cover your ass."

"I'm thinking the admiral wanted to settle his conscience, especially since you were attacked and targeted as a young woman. He wants to be sure you're protected. Just like your dad, the admiral carries his share of guilt."

"It's not necessary. Feeling bad never does any good."

He raised an eyebrow. "That sounds like something they teach in nanny school."

"Oh, my God, you're right. I sound like Mary Poppins."

"At least you get to fly."

"But I don't want to be a turn-of-the-century spinster who takes care of other people's kids." Those words were truer than he would ever know. "I'm changing my ringtone."

The waiter appeared and rattled off a list of special dishes ranging from chicken paprika to schnitzel and kraut. Without having to worry about watching the kids, she could choose adventurous foods. She selected something with potatoes and something with venison that she'd never before heard of. And they both ordered beer from a huge selection.

"This dating ritual is a little bit fantastic," she said. "I usually don't drink."

"Glad to oblige."

"I have an idea." She was still thinking about security and the cache. "We should do some crime solving. We're sitting in the middle of this great big web of intrigue and spies."

"So you're not Mary Poppins anymore."

"I never was."

"Now you're Nancy Drew."

"We might as well try to figure it out."

"It's not the worst idea I've ever heard," he said. "The anti-conspiracy people think the cache is in Prescott's house, and we're the only ones with access."

She hadn't forgotten that her father's name might be included in the cache. When it was located, he might be in danger. She wanted to find it, to end this threat. "The problem is that we're not cops. We don't have the authority to make people talk to us."

"But we hear a lot."

His knowing glance sparked her enthusiasm. In her role as nanny, nobody paid much attention to her. She never ever eavesdropped, but she couldn't help overhearing things. She knew that the handsome Agent Collier was having an affair with his fifteen-years-older CIA boss with the sexy shoulder-baring dress. She'd heard a couple of captains talking about someone else who had been fired. His name was Ackerman. Where had she heard that name before?

Their waiter returned with a basket of warm, fragrant bread and two frosted mugs filled with the restaurant's brand of beer brewed with local hops.

"These drinks are from the two gentlemen sitting by the window."

She looked over and saw Hank Grossman and Sam Bertinelli. What were the NSA agents doing here?

Chapter Fourteen

Mason noticed that Grossman and Bertinelli had only a couple of beers on their table—no leftover plates from dinner—and their silverware sat neatly on their linen napkins. They hadn't been in the restaurant for long, had probably arrived within minutes of when he and Lexie got here. Had the NSA agents been following them?

Lexie waved to them across the dining room and smiled. "Should we go over and talk to them?"

"If we don't," he said, "they'll come to us, plant themselves in chairs and refuse to leave."

"I don't want to spend my date with Grossman." She popped to her feet. "Also, this is an opportunity to investigate."

Mason wasn't the sort of guy who leaped before he looked. Jumping feetfirst into an investigation without considering the information they needed might be dangerous. "Be careful."

She shrugged. "It's just Grossman and Bertinelli."

Her cavalier attitude came from having high-ranking officers and federal agents passing through the Prescott home. Most people would be plenty scared if confronted with two men who worked for the National Security Agency. A little fear was smart. Either of these agents could be involved with the AC-CD group. They might know more about the Damascus Cache than they admitted in the meetings. Mason considered it likely that they had information they hadn't shared. The NSA had more covert ops than any other US intelligence service, both at home and abroad.

He followed Lexie across the half-full dining room and waited while she gave each of the NSA agents a hug. Mason shook hands. He nodded to Grossman and saved his comment for Bertinelli, who was by far the less offensive of the two. "I'm surprised to see you gentlemen here. This place has a reputation for being romantic."

"German food?" Grossman answered for his partner, pulling a frown and holding his nose in a not-so-subtle indication that he wasn't a fan of the cuisine. "There's nothing sexy about kraut."

"We came for the beer," Bertinelli said. He seemed nervous, as though he'd been caught in a lie. It pleased Mason to have that effect. "This place has a great selection of beer."

"I wasn't aware that you were staying in the area," Mason said. "What are you working on?"

Grossman slouched down in his chair. Though the waiter had poured some of his beer into a glass, he drank from the bottle. "I could ask the same question, Mason. What made you come back to town?"

He rested his hand on Lexie's shoulder. "We're on a date."

"That's real sweet," Grossman said in the exasperated tone he might use to say *I've got a flat tire*. His patience for civil conversation was just about spent, which was sad because it hadn't taken much to wear him down. Pretty soon they'd be hearing the full-out, probably obnoxious truth about why the NSA was in town and why they'd been following Mason's car. Good old sloppy Hank wouldn't be able to keep his mouth shut.

Bertinelli straightened his posture. He was more corporate in his attitudes, more economical with his words. But it was obvious that he didn't like playing a cat-and-mouse game, trying to figure out what the other guy was doing without asking a direct question. He reached up to his throat to adjust his necktie, but he wasn't wearing one. He had on a pullover sweater and a shirt with a button-down collar.

He fiddled with the buttons. "We heard you had some excitement at the house this afternoon."

"We did," Lexie said with the sweetest of smiles. "Who did you hear that from?"

"I can't remember. Maybe the guy at the gas station. Was there an accident at the house?"

"It's all taken care of," she said.

"Perhaps we could help," Bertinelli returned.

"The fire department was terrific," she said.

"It sounds dangerous," he said.

"We have things under control."

"Never hurts to have someone else check it out."

The two of them were lobbing comments back and

forth like a tennis match. Mason was pretty sure that Bertinelli wanted to wangle an invitation to the house so he could take a look around for himself. Mason didn't know what motivated Lexie, but she appeared to be enjoying herself. Her cheeks were pink, and her dark eyes glistened.

"That's enough," Grossman grumbled. "We all know what's going on here. We've been running surveillance on the house."

"Shocking," Lexie said.

"We saw the fire department and followed them back into town to observe their use of the blast chamber, which was very groovy."

Mason had figured the detonation would be fun; watching stuff blow up usually was. He wouldn't have used the word *groovy*, though. "You followed us here tonight."

Grossman looked over at his junior partner. "I told you he picked up on the tail."

"I don't think so. I was careful." Bertinelli looked hopefully toward Mason. "Did you see me?"

Mason didn't want to squash this last grasp at competence. "I didn't see you following, but I knew you were surveilling. Your arrival here is too coincidental."

Lexie stamped her foot. In her little cowgirl boots, she was adorable. "Why were you watching us and following us?"

"We've got no leads," Bertinelli said. "The CIA team didn't find anything that would lead us to the cache. None of our informants know anything, which isn't surprising, because most of them are in the Middle East."

"Yeah, it's a problem." Grossman took a long glug of his beer. "There aren't many spies or snitches in the high Rocky Mountains."

"You don't have to creep around the house," Lexie said.

"No?" Bertinelli's brows went up.

"I'll check with Helena and the admiral to make sure it's okay, and you can come over tomorrow around two in the afternoon. You can poke around to your heart's content."

As they returned to their table, he wished she hadn't been so generous with her hospitality. He didn't trust those two. From what Mason understood, the Damascus Cache was worth a lot of money to the right people—enough money to tempt someone like Grossman, who didn't have many years left as an active agent. Bertinelli might opt for a big payoff so he wouldn't have to be under Grossman's thumb.

Mason held Lexie's chair for her again. She turned her head to look up at him, and her grin widened. "That was fun."

He sat opposite her and sipped his beer from the frosted mug. "How was it fun?"

"For one thing, we were just too cool for school. We were, like, good cop and bad cop."

"Which one were you?"

"I'd like to say I was the bad cop, but I kind of invited them over to the house."

The idea of this cheerful, open-faced woman being a stern interrogator tickled him. "And you'll probably feed them cookies and milk."

"I'd like to point out that my method worked. Grossman admitted everything. I'm a little peeved that they've been snooping near the house with binoculars."

"If I were you, I'd make certain my curtains were always closed."

"What about you?"

If somebody was spying on him, Mason would stand at the window naked, waving and making rude gestures. "It's different with guys."

"I grew up with three brothers." She cocked her head to one side. Her gaze softened as she took a sip. The dark beer left a trace of froth on her lips. They seemed to be moving into the dating part of their evening, when the conversation turned more personal. "You just had the one brother, right?"

Matt was several years older, and Mason sometimes felt like an only child. He remembered when he was seven and saw the sign at Elitch Amusement Park that said you couldn't ride until you were a certain height.

"You must be this high." He held out his hand beside the table. "That's what I felt like as a kid. Matt was on the roller coaster, and I was on the sidelines waiting to grow. Then I did. And the age difference didn't matter."

"Did your family always live in Denver?"

"We spent a couple of years near San Francisco in Silicon Valley." His dad was a computer guy and had brushed up his skills with a stint at one of the big software companies. "How about you? Where have you lived?"

"Everywhere." She stretched her arms wide apart. "When you're a military brat, you get accustomed to shuffling from one place to another. Mostly, I've been in Texas. I'm a countrified woman. I grew up knowing how to ride, shoot and hunt. I'm not scared of snakes or spiders. And I love beef."

He liked her résumé, even though their childhoods didn't have much in common. He'd been a city kid who shot hoops, played sports, jogged and spent every Saturday morning with the chess club before discovering the gym. "I always wished I'd lived in the mountains. I'd have a whole different skill set."

"Like snowboarding and skiing."

"Rock climbing and kayaking."

She flashed one of her upturned smiles. "I'd like to learn how to do those things, but it's impossible while I'm being a nanny and need to watch out for the kids."

"Maybe while I'm here," he said, "we could learn together."

"I'd love to."

Their dinner was served. He couldn't argue with the portions. With the side dishes, including a container of pickles, the plates covered the whole surface of the table. He hadn't realized how hungry he was until he dug in. The beef was so tender it could be cut with a fork, and everything else—even the sauerkraut—was perfectly seasoned.

As their official date progressed, he learned more about her. Almost all her fond memories about her mother were from when she was a little girl. With her dad being deployed, her mom was lonely and her daughter was her only company. Her mom cried a lot, and Lexie tried to make her happy. She'd dance around with a goofy smile on her face or tell a joke or make up a nonsense song.

The two NSA agents came over and said goodbye before they left the restaurant. If they had the okay from the admiral and his wife, they'd come to the house tomorrow and make their own search for the cache.

"I should warn you," Lexie said to Bertinelli, "there's no way that Helena will let you go into the safe room, and I don't know how to open that door."

"Nobody has ever searched in there," he said.

"And nobody ever will unless Helena gives the okay." Big smile. "I don't think any judge will issue a search warrant for Admiral Prescott's private papers."

"Is that what's in there?"

She shrugged. "Could be."

As soon as the agents left, he reached across the table and took her hand. "We're going to search in the safe room tomorrow morning, aren't we?"

"Absolutely. It feels sneaky to do that to Bertinelli. He's not a bad guy."

"We don't know that. Don't know hardly anything about him."

"I do." She squeezed his fingers and reclaimed her hand. "Sam Bertinelli with his neat black hair and pretty hazel eyes wanted to go out with me, and I got curious about him. He's from Chicago, was an accountant for an oil exploration company before he joined the NSA and is twice divorced, no kids. He's also forty-seven, which is old enough to be my father. He was annoyed when I told him no. Then he pushed, and I hinted very subtly that the age difference bothered me. And then he was seriously angry."

"Gee, I wonder why."

Her cute smile twisted into an evil smirk. Sweet little Lexie wasn't a wide-eyed innocent. "Age isn't the only reason I didn't want to date him. There was a whole list of problems."

"I hope you're not holding any of those nasty bomblets for me. Maybe you hate men with blond hair. Or you never date guys whose first names start with *M*."

"I don't *enjoy* rejecting guys." There was a dark undertone to her voice, a mixture of anger and sadness. "But I don't see any point in getting started with a relationship that can never work."

"Not every relationship is going to end in marriage."

"I know." She scowled. "There are a million different kinds of relationships. Friends. Colleagues. Coworkers. You and I could be partner detectives."

"A lot of possibilities," he said. But there was one relationship he wanted with her. Pure and simple, one word, he wanted to be her lover.

EVER SINCE THE CRASH, Lexie had preferred vehicles with substance. Mason's ten-year-old Land Rover fit the bill. Leaning back in the passenger's seat, she felt a pleasant sense of security that wasn't entirely due to the muscular SUV wrapped around her. Mason would keep her safe. He was her protector.

She noticed that he was taking a different route back to the house and wasn't using his GPS device. "Do you think Grossman and Bertinelli are trying to follow us again?"

"Probably not."

"Why are you going this way? It's longer."

"Since I'm going to be here for a couple of weeks, it's useful for me to know my way around."

She gazed through the window at the twinkling lights of Aspen to her left in the distance. Though it was just after nine o'clock, there wasn't much traffic outside town. An occasional car or truck zipped past the Rover on the two-lane road. A truck had been following them for a few miles, but when Mason made a left, the truck stayed on the main road.

He drove into a wide, rocky canyon with cute little cabins on either side. She lowered her window so she could hear the burble of the narrow creek that had dictated the winding path of this road.

"What's this creek called?" he asked.

"It's the Little Wapiti. That's the Shawnee word for elk." She felt another grin coming on. "Actually, it means white rump."

"So if you told the kids you were going to spank them on their little wapitis…"

"Oh, I've told them that before. I never could bring myself to hit them. The threat is usually enough. You know what's crazy? I kind of miss the little beasties."

"That's not crazy. You love those kids, even the twins."

"I guess I do."

Casually chatting, they drove out of the canyon into the open expanse of Henscratch Valley. In the distance, the looming hills, dark pines and jagged rocks seemed alive in the shifting shadows and moonlight. It was a beautiful night, and she realized that she was having a good time. This date was a success. The food was good. The conversation was interesting. Would it end with a kiss? Should she invite him into her bedroom?

The Rover glided onto a section of road that zigzagged up the side of a cliff in sharp hairpin turns. Mason checked his rearview mirror. "Damn."

A ripple of fear went through her. "What is it?"

"The truck behind us. It's the third time I've seen him."

"Are you sure?" She turned and stared out the back window. A filthy truck was two car lengths behind them. "Lots of people drive trucks around here."

"Look at the license plate."

She wriggled around in her seat as much as she could without unfastening the seat belt. "I can't see it."

"Because he's covered the number with mud. On the front and back. Unidentifiable, he's just another beat-up old truck."

And the driver wants to kill us.

Chapter Fifteen

Remembered terror from her first devastating car crash sluiced through her veins and joined with a newer version of fear. Not again, not another crash.

Mason pushed the accelerator, and the Rover responded, leaping forward in a burst of speed. Though the narrow asphalt road ascended on a steep incline, their vehicle seemed to be going faster. They gained traction. The rear end fishtailed as they took the first of three tight curves.

The landscape whirled past her like a kaleidoscope. Her mouth was open to scream, but she couldn't make a sound. Her throat constricted, strangled by fear. Her heart thumped hard against her rib cage.

Even faster than the first curve, Mason swiveled the Rover around the second. The tires skidded but only a bit. He had control. He was a better driver than she'd ever been. With Mason at the wheel, they might survive.

If she had a choice, she might want to die rather than going through the physical agony of another bone-wrenching crash with injuries on top of injuries and days of constant surgeries. They said what didn't kill you made you stronger. Not true. Not for her.

It had taken every shred of her willpower to get through her painful physical therapy. She'd used up her lifetime allotment of courage battling the naysayers who told her she'd never walk again. But she would never choose death. She couldn't do that to her father.

There was only one more hairpin on this stretch. The vehicle behind them was so close that his headlights flashed in the Rover's rearview mirror and blinded her. Her hands flew up to cover her eyes. She couldn't bear to watch.

The Rover took the final curve at a fearsome speed. At the same time, the truck bumped the fender. They skidded and drifted across the center line. She heard gravel from the shoulder kick up and batter the undercarriage. Then the Rover straightened out.

Mason was driving so fast that she didn't dare peek at the speedometer, but she dropped her hands to her lap. "Is he gone?"

"Not yet."

The upper ridge of this cliff was above timberline; there were no trees blocking her view when she turned to look for the truck. He'd fallen back quite a distance. "Is something wrong with his truck?"

"It'd be a damn shame," Mason said, "if he damaged his vehicle while he was trying to kill us."

Her pulse was still racing, and she was breathing in frantic gasps. But they'd made it this far. She had reason to hope.

"What happens on the road ahead?" he asked. "It looks like we're headed into a forest."

"The trees are close on both sides of the road. It's a gradual descent, not a lot of huge drop-offs."

"I don't want to get trapped in there."

"No?"

"Hell, no. We're taking the fight to him."

But she didn't want to fight. She was happy to see the truck falling even farther back. "It looks like he's given up."

"Brace yourself."

The Rover rounded a gentle curve. For a moment, their vehicle was hidden from the truck behind a rocky mound. Mason tap-danced between the accelerator and brake, throwing them into a spin in the middle of the road. The Rover came around one hundred and eighty degrees. He killed the headlights. They sat and waited for the truck to approach.

She had no trouble screaming, "Are you insane?"

"This time, we'll get him."

"'This time'? What do you mean 'this time'? It's not the same guy who hit me before."

It couldn't be. That was in a different area, at a different time. The first attack was for different reasons. Why was Mason putting the two together?

She saw the headlights approaching.

Mason revved the engine.

She couldn't believe he'd try to take out a truck with his SUV. Land Rovers were sturdy, but this wasn't a Hummer. On the hopeful side, it was possible that Mason knew exactly where to strike the truck to disable it. His one-hundred-and-eighty-degree turn had been impressive.

He stopped revving and sat back in his seat as his hands dropped from the steering wheel. "It's not him," he said.

A Volkswagen bug chugged around the curve and kept on going. She asked. "How did you know?"

"The beams from the headlights were too low for a truck." He turned toward her. "We need to go after him. Keep your eyes open. He might have pulled off on a side road."

"No." She reached over and grabbed his arm as though restraining him could stop the car. "This is where we need to remember that we aren't federal agents or detectives. Here is where people like you and me have to back down and let the police take over."

"The guy who attacked us—the guy in the truck— is a lead. We can't let him get away."

"What if he's waiting for us? What if he's armed?"

Mason patted the shoulder holster he wore under his sports jacket. "So am I."

Turning her head away from him, she folded her arms below her breasts and stared straight ahead through the windshield. Arguing wouldn't do a bit of good. Mason was as stubborn as the men in her family. Once they got a course of action set in their minds, they couldn't be stopped.

He tapped the accelerator, and the Rover rolled slowly forward. The car eased around the edge of the mound. The high mountain road stretched before them. There wasn't another vehicle or human being in sight.

Nothing but grasses and junipers and a single lodgepole pine that reached up toward the Big Dipper.

Instead of taking up the chase, Mason made a three-point turn. The Rover was headed back toward the house. "You're right. I have no business chasing after that guy."

She was grateful that he'd changed his mind. "Thank you for listening to me, for hearing me."

"I'm not a cop. It's wrong for me to put you in danger. My job is to keep you safe."

He activated his hands-free phone and called the chief investigating officer from the Aspen police, whom he'd met at the hotel.

She sat in silence, chewing her lower lip and wishing that she didn't like Mason as much as she did. *I don't want to hurt you. Don't make me hurt you.* The near crash reminded her of the past and made many things clear to her. After dinner, she'd been pleased with their date, thinking about their relationship and wondering if this evening should end with a kiss…or something more interesting. But that was wrong. Intimacy wasn't an option.

A committed connection with Mason would never work. She couldn't provide him with a family, and she knew he wanted kids. A bright energy emanated from him when he talked about his brother and growing up with his buddies Dylan and Sean. Mason was comfortable with the Prescott kids. He couldn't help chuckling when he was around little Princess Stella, and he was cool with the older boys. A natural-born family man.

She glanced over at him. He was watching the road

and talking on the phone, describing the truck that looked like hundreds of other trucks in this area. There'd be a dent in the truck's front fender, passenger side and in the grille. He gave their location with pinpoint precision.

He would have made a good cop, but TST Security probably paid better and he had more freedom. The downside of TST was getting stuck with a prickly client like her. She needed to end this budding whatever-it-was right now. It was the smart thing to do.

WHEN THEY ARRIVED at the Prescott house, Mason was glad he'd insisted on parking in one of the four spaces attached to the house. Climbing the hill from the larger parking garage would have meant unnecessary exposure. The guy in the truck might have a cohort watching the house, a sniper.

But it seemed unlikely, because none of the attacks had been lethal. The charge on the bomblets had been too small to cause serious damage. The truck had given up too easily. The only thing accomplished by the chase on the mountain roads was scaring Lexie half to death. He'd watched as her fear rose up and overwhelmed her. He'd seen her pain.

When he parked in the garage and the lights came on, she had her seat belt off in seconds. She reached for the door handle.

"Wait," he said.

"What for?" The harsh overhead light made the freckles stand out on her face. Her usually sparkling eyes were dull and tired.

"Just wait."

"Fine."

He came around to her side of the Rover and opened the door for her. "I won't pretend this date is ending the way I'd hoped, but it doesn't have to be all bad."

"I agree." Her forehead pinched in an unfamiliar scowl. "We're going to be together for a while, like it or not. Might as well try to get along."

"I wanted to say…" This wasn't an apology. He wasn't sorry that his first impulse had been to go after the bad guys. "I can't begin to understand the pain you suffered in that first crash. You're a brave woman, a strong woman. I respect you and your opinions. And I never should have suggested chasing down that truck."

Her features softened a bit. "I know why you were tempted. I'm as anxious as you to have this threat over with."

She left his car and walked toward the house. At the entry, Mason punched in the numerical code that was synced with all the other security systems. Feedback indicated that nothing had been disturbed, but he would make a visual sweep before they went to bed. The attack on the road meant he needed to step up his regular procedures. "Lieutenant Hough from the Aspen police is going to stop by tonight to take our statements."

"Can't it wait until morning?"

"He wants to get the details while they're fresh in mind. My car insurance company can wait."

After they moved from the garage to the house, he rearmed the alarm and followed her on a winding trek through the huge house to the kitchen.

She tossed a comment over her shoulder. "How are

you going to explain to the insurance people that you couldn't exchange information at the scene of the accident?"

"Maybe they have a box I can check for lunatic psycho." He shrugged. "The Rover has been battered worse than this. She's a tough little car."

"She?"

"Rhonda," he said, "as in 'Rhonda, you look so fine.'"

She went to the fridge, got waters for both of them and placed the plastic bottles on the counter. Some of the tension had left her shoulders. Her posture was more relaxed.

He hated to do anything that would upset her again, but he couldn't let this slide. "I'm going to have to notify the admiral about this."

"I suppose."

"You know what that means."

"My dad."

"You have to call him, Lexie. He nearly went berserk the last time he thought you were in danger. A car chase seems even more directed, more personal."

She pinned him with a sharp gaze. "Is that what you think?"

"There's something weird about it." He pulled a stool up to the counter and sat. "How does running us off the road connect with the admiral and the Damascus Cache?"

"It might have been a warning. Like the first time I got crashed."

"But there's no clear message. What kind of threat is it to attack the nanny and a bodyguard?"

As her scowl deepened, her freckled nose twitched. The woman couldn't help being adorable, even when she was deeply worried. "I don't suppose the admiral would be convinced to talk because you and I were hostages."

"He's got six kids. Any one of them would be a better hostage."

"Maybe not the twins." She tried to grin, but the attempt failed.

"Your dad might have some ideas," he said. "I'm sure he knows more about your first crash than anyone else."

"You can forget that line of questioning. I will call my dad and inform him that someone bumped your fender, but I'm not going into any details about the cache."

"Didn't you say his name was in it?"

"Yes, but…"

"Do you want me to call him?"

Her face lit up with pure, beautiful relief. The veil lifted from her eyes. Her smile came back. "I should be able to take care of this myself. Let me think about it."

"Think fast," he said. "It's ten o'clock here and an hour later in Austin."

Taking his water bottle, he went down the hall to the richly furnished office and sat behind the desk. It wasn't so much that he needed privacy, but he wanted Lexie to have some space to think. The call to her father was going to be difficult, no matter who made it.

He took out his phone. He wasn't pleased to be sending separate text messages to the admiral and Helena. This was his second message in one day—his first day on the job. The way he saw his security position was to keep the house and Lexie protected and not to bother the people who hired him. The Prescotts shouldn't have to worry, and he felt like an alarmist when he texted them about every little thing. But when emergency personnel, like cops and firemen, came to the house, the Prescotts needed to be informed.

He sent the texts, leaned back in the swivel chair and put his feet on the desk blotter. He waited.

Lexie appeared in the open doorway. "Make the call."

Chapter Sixteen

"Sergeant Major DeMille, this is Mason Steele from TST Security. We've never met, but you might have known my brother. He was a marine, stationed in Afghanistan. His name was Matthew Steele."

"Sorry, I don't recall the name." Lexie's dad cleared his throat. "I'll tell you what, young man. I'm giving you ten seconds to explain why you called in the middle of the night."

"I work for Admiral Edgar Prescott as a bodyguard." He put the call on speakerphone so Lexie could hear. "I'm at the Prescott home in Aspen with your daughter."

"Is she all right?" The anxiety was evident.

Mason imagined DeMille jolting forward, fully awake. "Yes, but there was an incident earlier tonight."

"Put her on the phone. What did you say your name was? Mason Steele? Listen up, Mason Steele, you put my daughter on the phone right now."

No doubt about it, Sergeant Major Danny DeMille was an intimidating person, a real hard-ass. But Mason had already backed down for Lexie and wasn't in the mood to do the same for her dad. "Your daughter asked me to explain."

"Did she, now?"

Mason started right in. "After dinner, we were driving back to the Prescott home in my Land Rover."

"What year is your Rover?"

"It's a 2003 Land Rover Discovery with the square top."

"Nice, that's a car that looks like a car."

Why was DeMille being chatty about vehicles? Trying to be friendly? No way. He might be trying to distract Mason. Or he might be nervous. This conversation about his daughter had been a long time coming.

Mason looked over at Lexie. At the far end of the tan leather sofa, she was curled up in a ball with her knees pulled up to her chin. Her eyes were squeezed shut, but she was still listening.

"Driving back to the house," Mason continued, "we came to a series of hairpin curves. A truck pulled up behind us."

"Had you noticed being followed before that?"

"Yes, sir, but the truck was maintaining a safe distance. This was a narrow mountain road with no exits. Evasive driving tactics were not possible."

"Anything's possible," he growled, "if you've got the guts to do it."

"The truck was on my bumper, going too fast. At the curve, he smacked my rear fender. I recovered and we reached an open stretch of road. I pulled far ahead."

"The truck didn't keep up?"

"No, sir, he fell back. When I got to a place where I

could turn, I did a one-eighty and got ready to ambush this guy. But he was gone."

"Did you pursue?"

"My job is to keep your daughter and the Prescott home safe." He nodded to Lexie, acknowledging that the retreat was her idea. She didn't see him. Her eyes were still closed. "We immediately came back to the house, where the security system is fully activated. The police will come here to take our statements."

"Well, Mason, it sounds like you're doing a fine job. Put my Franny on. She's listening to this call, isn't she? Francine Alexandra DeMille, you pick up the phone."

Mason didn't give her the chance. He wasn't letting this guy off the hook until he got some answers. "What can you tell me about the Damascus Cache?"

"Sorry, son, that information is above your pay grade. It's none of your business."

"When somebody tries to run me off the road, it becomes my business. Why would somebody who's interested in the cache come after Lexie? Could there be a connection to her earlier accident?"

"Whoa, there. I never said these two incidents were connected. You're jumping to conclusions."

"She knows." He paused for a moment, allowing those words to sink in. "Lexie knows that the first accident was a warning to the intelligence community in the Middle East. She knows that she was hurt to prove a point. Helena Prescott sat her down and had a heart-to-heart talk."

"Damn it, Helena had no right to shoot off her mouth."

"Your daughter has a right to know." Her eyes were

open, staring at him. He couldn't tell if she was angry or on the verge of tears.

"It was my fault," DeMille said. "My baby girl was almost killed because of my job."

"Like father, like daughter. Lexie blames herself for taking you away from the work that you love." He could have been angry with these two. They were so busy trying to protect each other that they didn't realize how much they were hurting themselves. "I've never known a family so anxious to take responsibility. You and your daughter must love each other very much."

"She's the light of my life." His voice caught, and he exhaled a ragged breath. "Tell me the truth, Mason. Is there any way I could help if I came to Aspen?"

"The investigation has run into one snafu after another. Prescott has no idea where the cache might be, and the Anti-Conspiracy Committee for Democracy thinks he's lying and has the cache hidden in the house. The CIA has made a search. The NSA is coming tomorrow." He decided not to mention the bomblets on the roof. "There's a serious lack of evidence."

"You're grasping at straws, young man. That's why you asked me about connections between Lexie's accident and this truck that bumped your fender."

"The truck was in serious pursuit. But he quit after one tap. Why?"

"The real question is, why do you think I'd know?"

"Because you probably know more about Lexie's first accident than anyone."

"You're right about that. I researched the hell out of the accident, got real serious about forensics and watched every interview with every suspect," he rambled on, describing a desperate yet futile investigation where he was riding the detectives every step of the way. "As you know, they never caught the bastard who did it."

"Did you work up a profile?"

"You know I did."

"Will you fax it to me?"

"I'll do better than that, Mason. I'll make a copy of the whole file and ship it express. There might be some detail that helps your investigating."

"Technically, I'm not an investigator."

"But you're in this up to your elbows." He chuckled. "Now will you put my daughter on the phone?"

Mason handed over the phone and left the room. As he closed the door, he heard her say, "I love you, too."

AFTER THE BEST talk she'd ever had with her dad, Lexie came out of the office to find Mason. She checked the time on her phone. She and her dad had only spoken for fifteen minutes, but she felt deeply loved by a man whose gruff manner couldn't completely conceal his open heart.

Not in the kitchen. "Mason? Where are you?"

"Upstairs."

She skipped down the hall and across the foyer toward the sweeping staircase that climbed to the second floor. Mason was unpacking the few belongings he'd brought with him in the best, largest bedroom suite in the house. Twice the size of the other bedrooms, this guest suite also had a sitting room with a huge sofa and chairs. There was even a desk by the window. The decor was a classic southwestern style. Two woven rugs with deep blues, sienna and turquoise decorated the floor. The rough-hewn coffee table held a round, fat cactus.

"Nice room," she said.

"I thought so."

"You think you're pretty hot stuff."

"There's a reason I'm taking this room. We're both going to sleep in here."

"Me? With you?" She didn't dare! Being that close to him would be too tempting, and she was determined to keep their relationship at the friend level. "I don't think so."

"It's not a choice," he said. "I can't protect you if we're sleeping in separate rooms."

"Oh, please. Do you really think somebody is going to get past all this security and sneak up on me?"

"After talking to your dad, I'm not going to take that chance."

Her father had that effect. "Yeah, if anything happens to me, you're a dead man."

He pointed to the extra-long king-size bed. "There's plenty of room. You could fit all the Prescott kids and a small pony in that bed."

On this issue, she had to put her foot down. No way were they sleeping in the same bed. "There's the sofa. If you insist on being in the same room, you can sleep there."

"I suppose you know there's a tub with massaging water jets in the bathroom."

"On occasion, I've been known to take a nice, long soak in there. It uses less water than the hot tub."

"And you can be naked." He wiggled his eyebrows. "How did the rest of the conversation with your dad go?"

"Great! I forgave him and vice versa. He's still worried about me, but not so much with you being here. He's already looked up TST Security on his computer, and he believes you're qualified."

"Good to know."

"He checked out your photo. Likes your buzz cut."

"I don't wear it this way to impress retired marines," he said. "I like it short in the summer because it's efficient and cool when I'm outside."

"Apparently, there's a photo of you and your Land Rover on the TST website. He said to tell you it was a good vehicle."

"Ha!" He sank onto the sofa that would be his bed. "Your dad is a sneaky old codger. That's why he was asking about my car. First thing he did when we started talking was to look me up."

"'Sneaky old codger'?" She nodded. "That would be accurate."

From downstairs, she heard the familiar doorbell chime: "Yo ho ho, and a bottle of rum." She left the room. "That must be the cops."

"Lieutenant Hough," he reminded her. "Be nice to the guy. He's going out of his way for us."

"DON'T GO INTO the house," the leader said. "That is a direct order, Tony."

"What if I could slip in there for a few minutes and

plant some bugs?" He'd had listening devices all over the house before the CIA came through and cleaned them out like a bunch of high-tech maids. "Or a camera."

"I don't want you to take the risk of getting caught. I need you. You're my best man."

"Damn right, I am."

"But if you ever pull a stunt like you did earlier, I'll get rid of you. No more easy paydays. No more fun."

"But there was no harm done."

"You ignored my orders. Never do that again."

Tony ended the call and dropped his glowing cell phone on the seat of the used sedan he'd bought in Denver when he knew he'd be spending time in the mountains. He didn't want to lose his easy paycheck.

Chasing down the bodyguard's Land Rover wasn't the first time Tony had disobeyed a direct order from the leader. There had been the incident in Montreal when he was supposed to grab a Russian drug lord off the street and rough him up. The guy was a loudmouth jerk. Tony had shut him up for good.

Ultimately, it turned out to be a good thing that he'd eliminated the threat from the Russian, but the leader had been angry when it happened. The same way he was mad at Tony for crashing into the Land Rover when he was only supposed to keep an eye on Lexie.

Tony hadn't set out to break the rules, hadn't planned it. He just couldn't stop himself.

When she and the bodyguard left the house, he'd been surprised. If Tony had been locked inside that mansion with a sexy little babe like Lexie, he wouldn't go anywhere. They had plenty of food, booze, a pool table, video games and a swimming pool. Hell, they even had their own movie theater in the basement.

He had watched them drive away. He didn't have to tail them because he'd already attached a GPS tracer to the bodyguard's car, but he followed, anyway. And he noticed another car watching. They were forming a damn parade.

That was when he got the idea of running them off the road. It'd be ironic. Five years ago, he'd almost killed Lexie with a car crash. It was one of his first assignments from the leader. At first, he thought the crash was a dumb idea. He'd told the leader that a bullet was more efficient, and he'd been right. She survived the accident. Apparently, that was the best outcome, after all. A bunch of the undercover ops and agents came to visit the sick little girl, and they could all imagine their family members going through a struggle like hers.

A year and a half ago, he'd arranged to meet her. He'd been expecting an invalid. At the very least, she'd be wheelchair bound or limping around on a cane. Instead, he found this energetic little fireball. She was hot. She was tough. And she owed her life to him.

He was ready to collect that debt. His first car accident failed to kill her. This one would succeed. If not, he had his rifle. He'd stolen a truck and waited. By the time they left the restaurant, he was pumped.

Making sure they didn't have another tail, he followed at a distance. At times, he let them get out of his sight and tracked them on the GPS. They wouldn't suspect a thing until…

Tony closed in at the first of the hairpin curves. That damn bodyguard was a good driver. His car was in control. When the first hit failed to even slow them down, Tony fell back. His plan was to wait for them to come to him.

He would have shot the bodyguard and kidnapped Lexie. But they never showed. Cowards.

The way he figured, she owed him one.

Chapter Seventeen

The detective from the Aspen police was cordial and efficient and offered very little hope of finding the driver who ran into them. The truck might have been stolen. Or the dirt obscuring the license plate might be legitimate grime. It could be local teens messing around.

It was frustrating not to get answers, but she understood. Everything about this case was baffling. Top agents in the CIA and NSA were stumped. Why should she expect local law enforcement to figure it out? It was clear that the Aspen police chief was backing away from this mess as quickly as possible. The five guys who were arrested at the hotel had already been transferred to federal custody and were being charged with attempted terrorism…or something like that.

After the lieutenant had recorded her statement, her interest waned to a mere sliver. Mason and the cop went into the garage to look at his crumpled fender, and she didn't bother to tag along. Though this hadn't been a physically taxing day, not compared with her usual chasing around with the kids, which kept her on her feet, she was tired. Today weighed heavily on her emotions.

From her first trickle of fear when Mason arrived to finding the bomblets to the car chase that had been horribly reminiscent of what happened to her five years ago. She recalled what Mason had said. *This time, we'll get him.* What did he mean by that? It couldn't be the same driver, it couldn't be.

After they'd said good-night to the lieutenant, she trudged upstairs. Mason followed, making sure that she was going to bed in the large guest suite instead of her own cozy room.

As he watched, she dropped her nightshirt—a gift from Princess Stella that was covered in pink unicorns—at the lower end of the king-size bed and pulled back the gazillion-thread-count mauve duvet. "You know, movie stars have slept on this mattress. Famous people, fabulous people."

"Anybody I'd know?"

"I don't know. What kind of movies do you like?"

"I like when stuff blows up." He gave her a sheepish grin. "And zombies, yeah, I like zombies."

She named two older actors who starred in a zombie franchise. "And we've had vampires. And aliens."

"That must be fun."

"Not so much," she said. "These people are Helena's friends. They like visiting here because of the skiing. Since I'm not much of a skier or snowboarder, they have more in common with the guy who drives them to the slopes."

"Skiing is one of those things you never learned in

Texas," he said. "I'm not great, but I could show you a couple of moves."

"Too bad there's no snow."

"But there will be in a couple of months," he said. "Winter always comes around too fast."

"I hope you're not planning to stay here as my bodyguard for the changing of the seasons."

"Maybe I wouldn't be your bodyguard."

"Stop!" She threw up a palm. "I don't make long-range plans. Leave the future to take care of itself."

She snatched up her nightshirt and stomped into the bathroom. Too bad she'd forgotten her toothpaste and brush from her bathroom down the hall. Her dramatic exit was ruined when she stomped past him again.

When she returned with her bathroom supplies, he was sprawled out on the sofa with his long legs stretched out straight in front of him. "I have an idea for our investigation, Nancy Drew. You want to hear it?"

"Toothpaste first."

"It's always something," he grumbled.

She returned to the room, went to the desk by the window and closed the laptop computer she'd placed there earlier. Then she perched on the desk chair, which just happened to be the farthest spot away from his sofa. "Okay, what's this big idea?"

"Let's agree that we can trust the admiral. That means he's not hiding the cache and hasn't seen it in years."

"Okay." She liked the way he laid things out logically.

"But the AC-CD group is certain the cache is in this house. That means someone else brought it to the house. And there's an informant who talked to AC-CD."

"This all makes sense," she said. "So we have to figure out who planted it and find the mole. When you break the problem down, the solution seems easy."

"Then you add in the dozens of people who have visited this house recently. You estimated that there were thirty in the past four days."

She started taking a tally on her fingers. The admiral and his entourage, including Josh and bodyguards, had flitted through on their way to the Pentagon. Helena's hairdresser and stylist came by before she left for California, because there was no way she intended to face her hunky ex-husband without looking fabulous. The older kids had had friends over. There had been a playdate for the little ones with three friends and their parents. The cook and her assistant received food and wine deliveries. The maids came through on Wednesday. The housekeeper had an appointment with an accountant. "At least thirty."

"We need a chart like the one downstairs that you made to keep track of the family's vacations. It'd show who came to visit, how long they stayed and if there was overlapping timing."

"I can use records from the housekeeper and the cook to put that together." His idea was proactive, and she'd much rather be working on that than sitting and waiting for the next weird assault. "I see only one problem with this. After we have everybody listed, how do we know who's guilty?"

"One step at a time." He hopped off the sofa and

crossed the room to the desk where she was sitting. He leaned down and lightly kissed her forehead. "We'll take it one step at a time."

She wasn't sure if he was still talking about crime solving or their possible relationship.

Both, she hoped.

LEXIE WAS IN the middle of a nightmare, but she wasn't really scared because she knew she was asleep. The scenario was too obvious. A faceless driver dodged through a thick forest to chase her. He kept gunning the engine of his truck. *Vroom, vroom, vroom*. He was coming closer, and she was running but not really hard, not struggling. Then the scenery changed.

She was on a beach with the surf crashing and receding on hard sand. When she looked over her shoulder, the car was gone. A man was running toward her.

Even though he was far away, she recognized Mason's muscular shoulders and buzz haircut. He was running hard and wearing red trunks like the guys on *Baywatch*. *Vroom, vroom, vroom*. As Mason got closer, he was joined by members of the old cast, tanned men and gorgeous women in red suits. Over the sound of the surf, she could still hear the revving of the truck. *Vroom...*

She blinked and was awake. What did that dream mean? She was afraid of the car coming after her. That much was clear. But was she also afraid of having Mason pursue her? Or maybe her nightmare was about crime. Maybe it was telling her that David Hasselhoff was the faceless driver in the truck.

Squinting, she could see across the large room to the

sofa where Mason curled on his side, unable to stretch out all the way. In contrast, her body barely made a ripple under the duvet on the huge bed. It really wasn't fair for her to have all this wonderful space to spread out while he was cramped. She ought to offer to trade for the rest of the night.

She slipped from the covers. The big room was cool at night, which was good for sleeping but not running around. She padded across the woven Navajo rugs to his sofa. If he was sound asleep, it meant he wasn't uncomfortable, and she'd leave him there. *Let sleeping dogs lie.* His eyes were closed.

On tiptoe, she approached and leaned over him, hardly daring to breathe in case she woke him. His dark eyelashes made crescents above his heavy cheekbones. His jaw and mouth were relaxed, making his lips appear fuller and softer. Glancing down, she noticed that he wasn't wearing a shirt.

A shiver of awareness went through her. She wanted him, wanted to feel his warm flesh against hers. It had been over a year since she'd been intimate with a man, and she felt a familiar need.

Lexie had never been a prude. Maybe because she grew up around men, she'd never learned to play flirty games like other girls. She enjoyed sex, and she was surprised when others complained about how they never got satisfaction from the act. She did, multiple times. A low groan escaped her lips. She missed it.

His eyes popped open. Even in the darkness of the bedroom, that flash of blue was startling. Before she could do or say anything, he grabbed her and pulled her on top of him.

He kissed her. His arm encircled her. His large hand cradled the back of her skull, holding her so she couldn't move, couldn't escape while his mouth ravaged hers. Usually, she didn't think in those terms. *Ravage* wasn't a word she used, but there was nothing else she could call it when he was so demanding and so dominant.

It was purely impossible for her to hold back. She flung herself against his bare chest. He was so toasty warm. She kissed the hard column of his neck and the hollow of his throat while his musky scent coiled around her. She glided her fingers down his arm, tracing the ridges of his thick, hard muscles under his supple skin.

She groaned again, arched her back. His hands were all over her, pulling up her unicorn nightshirt. He almost reached her breast. She stopped breathing, waiting at the peak of anticipation.

Then…he stopped.

He opened his arms wide.

She scooted away from him so quickly that her bottom landed with a thud on the floor. She pushed her hair off her face and glared into the darkness. "What?"

"I didn't mean to grab you like that," he mumbled as he sat up on the sofa. "I thought I was dreaming."

If they had both been asleep, sex would have been appropriate. There would be no messiness, no strings attached and no thoughts of their potential for a future life together. "But we're not sleeping."

"What are you doing all the way over here?" he asked.

"I felt sorry for you, all squished up on the sofa."

"Thank you." Before she could say that she no longer had any qualms about making him sleep here, he was on the move. He threw off the sheets and blankets. She was glad to see that he wasn't sleeping naked, but had on gray jersey boxer shorts. He shivered once, acknowledging that it was chilly in here, and then he charged across the room. In seconds, he was under the duvet on the opposite side of the bed from hers.

He exhaled a huge sigh as he snuggled into the pillows. "Oh, yeah. This is heaven."

Though she couldn't see his face, she knew he was smiling. She couldn't interpret the meaning of a sigh, but she knew he was happy. And she didn't have the heart to throw him out.

As she got under her covers, she said, "You have to stay over there."

"Not a problem."

"I mean it, Mason. Don't come sneaking across the bed in the middle of the night."

To emphasize her words, she constructed a wall of pillows using the ones on the bed and running back and forth to the sofa.

When she had them all piled up, he peeked over the top. "Is this supposed to stop me?"

"It's supposed to get your attention," she said. "Then you'll notice that you're not sleeping and you'll stop yourself. Because you're a gentleman."

"Right," he drawled. "How is it that you don't have a custom-made chastity belt?"

She delivered a serious karate chop to the pillows. "I never needed one."

"Good night, Lexie."

She rearranged the duvet. With Mason in the bed—on the other side of the pillow wall—she fell asleep quickly and wasn't aware of any other bad dreams. When she woke, sunlight was streaming around the edges of the drapes. The digital clock showed the time as 7:22 a.m. She heard the thrum from the shower in the attached bathroom.

He'd interrupted her shower yesterday. Turnabout was fair play. She ought to sneak in there and steal all the towels. But no, she didn't want to encourage him.

Last night, their kiss had been accidental. At least, she could pretend that she'd never meant for it to happen, that she'd somehow been sleepwalking and had fallen on top of him. And all her groaning and groping was part of a nightmare where she was wrestling an octopus.

There was no excuse for that very hot, sexy kiss and embrace. She couldn't deny that she had wanted him. But she didn't need to mention it, either.

They were going to be spending a lot of time together over the next few weeks. She had to make sure their friendship didn't turn into anything more serious.

A romantic relationship would never work. Not only was there the whole issue of her not being able to have kids, but they were set on different paths in their lives.

He was determined to make TST Security a success.
She liked being a nanny.

There couldn't be anything between them.

Chapter Eighteen

Lexie marched resolutely to her bedroom, avoiding the temptation of lolling around in the king-size bed and watching Mason emerge from the shower with a towel slung around his hips. Nothing was going to happen between them. They were working together to find the cache. Other than that? *Nada.*

In her own small bathroom, she splashed water on her face, brushed her teeth using an extra brush she found in her cabinet and applied the tiniest bit of makeup. Just because she wasn't trying to seduce him, she didn't need to look like an escapee from one of those zombie movies he liked.

She made a mental note to tell him about the unique feature of the movie theater downstairs. Helena had wanted it to show films, but the admiral wanted a privacy room where no technology could reach him. He could flip a switch in the theater and create white noise so no one could listen with a bug. An invisible-to-the-naked-eye spectrum of light masked the presence of anyone in that room, and it could even fool infrared technology. Being able to disappear might come in handy.

She dragged a brush through her hair and pulled it up in a ponytail. For clothes, she put on sweats, a long-sleeve T-shirt and a fleece vest to ward off the morning coolness. Nothing sexy or cute about this outfit. Then she bounded downstairs to make coffee.

Mason beat her to it. He stood over the coffeemaker and muttered, "Come on, how long does it take? Come on."

She took a mug from the shelf and joined him at the counter. "I heard you in the shower. How'd you get dressed so fast?"

"I air dried."

That would have been fun to watch. It seemed that he was one of those people who took a while to wake up. One of her brothers was like that—half conscious for the first hour of the day, totally unaware and funny without knowing it. "You must really need your coffee."

He rubbed his hand against his jaw. "Didn't shave."

His stubble came in fast. She guessed that he could sprout a full beard in a week or so. Apparently, he'd gotten the memo about not dressing up. On top, he wore a University of Denver sweatshirt that had been red about ten years ago. The sleeves stopped above his elbow and looked as if they'd been torn off by a grizzly bear. He wore baggy gray shorts on the bottom. No socks. Beat-up black moccasins.

Though he appeared to be inches away from homeless, there was still something appealing about him.

The blond fur on his forearms and calves was probably longer than his buzz-cut hair, and she had a crazy urge to stroke him like a hound.

The coffeemaker was done, and she poured cups for both of them. He stumbled around the counter to a stool, sat and took a long sip. He scowled. "You're wide awake."

"Almost eight o'clock, it's time to get started. I should call the admiral and tell him about Grossman and Bertinelli coming here to search. Plus I'll report about the chase."

"Be sure to tell him that we talked to your dad."

"I will." That was her main reason for calling. Her talk with her dad had been great, and she didn't want Prescott calling him and saying anything that would make him worry.

"I texted both the admiral and Helena last night. You're aware of that, aren't you?"

"That was *your* business—bodyguard business. When I talk to them, it's more about family." She sipped her coffee. "And I want to get started on the charts we talked about."

His expression was blank. "Charts?"

She pointed to the listing on the wall that he'd used as an example last night. "We talked about this. The chart would show people who have been to the house, when they came, how long they stayed, et cetera. Then we can figure out who brought the cache here and hid it."

As she continued, he seemed to remember. He nodded, drank coffee and nodded faster.

"A spreadsheet for suspects," she said.

"And the room," he said. "You're going to open the safe room for me."

She wished he'd forget that little promise. To access the safe room, she needed to use Helena's personal computer. It felt like prying, and she was afraid of running across something private and secretive, like the time she'd accidentally opened the diary Helena had written when she and Prescott were dating. All doodled with hearts, everything was sweet and sexy and it was none of Lexie's business. But once she'd taken that first peek, she couldn't look away.

Mason finished his coffee and went down to the gym for a morning workout. Two hours later, she found him back in the kitchen, eating a bowl of granola cereal with a banana and, of course, more coffee. He looked like a new man. The stubble was gone, and he was dressed in layers for a spring day in Aspen with cargo shorts and hiking boots, a T-shirt on top and a plaid flannel over that.

"Wow," she said drily. "You look like the centerfold for an L.L.Bean catalog."

"Hey, this is how I dress. I've lived in Colorado for a very long time. I'm outdoorsy."

"Just keep telling yourself that, city boy."

His grin brightened the whole room. Then he shoveled in another spoonful of granola. "What have you got there?"

She flipped open her laptop. "I transferred records from the cook and the housekeeper to make a list of visitors for the past year. Taken one day at a time, it doesn't seem like much. But over a twelve-month period, there have been over three hundred people in the house."

"Can you break it down?"

"Already did. I eliminated locals, like delivery people and repairmen. Then I took out friends of the kids and social groups, like a charity board who met here to discuss their event."

"Did you keep those people on a separate list?"

"As a matter of fact, I did." It had taken some effort to compile these names, and she didn't want to dump them until they were sure they didn't need them. "Why?"

"A delivery person who appears innocent might be your faceless driver who tried to crash into us. Or might have planted the bomblets on the roof. Or could be searching for the cache."

She hadn't considered that possibility. Randy, the local florist who could whip up a centerpiece at a moment's notice, took on a more sinister aspect. How did he know Helena's favorite flowers were white roses?

She scrolled through the pages. "The last two groups are the movie people and the government types."

"Helena's friends." He turned his right palm up as though he could hold these directors, actors and the starving writers as one group. "And Edgar's associates."

"I've been concentrating on the government types," she said. "There's not much I know about their backgrounds. It might be helpful to figure out who knows who."

"No problem. The computer guy at TST can take care of the research."

"Dylan," she said, recalling the lanky guy with the ponytail at the hotel. "He seems decent."

"A real peach."

He scraped the last nibble of cereal into his mouth, took his bowl to the sink, rinsed it and put it in the dishwasher. The easy way he went through these motions made her think that he was in the habit of cleaning up after himself. Mason was good at planning ahead, a trait that suited him well as a bodyguard. And he was tidy, almost obsessively.

The man was perfect husband material. Too bad she wasn't looking for a spouse.

"Okay," he said, "let's do the safe room."

MASON FOLLOWED HER up the stairs to the bedroom suite that belonged to the admiral and his lady. It wasn't any bigger than the bedroom they'd slept in last night, but the Prescotts' room had a sultry, sexy aura. The colors were deeper, richer, and there were lots of subtle personal touches. Helena's fancy bottles of lotions and perfumes mingled with his clothing brushes, aftershave and an opened bottle of single malt. There were chocolates in a container that looked like the Eiffel Tower and a cigar humidor with a couple of Cubans. She had a book on her side of the bed. From the steamy cover, it had to be a romance.

That was what the guest room lacked: romance. It was clean and attractively furnished, but there was no passion. By contrast, the Prescotts' suite was loaded with character. There were two desks by windows on either side of the bed. Helena's desk was strewn with knickknacks, including three acting awards, and her computer. Her husband had a filing cabinet on wheels. Mason went over and flipped the lid open. It was jam-packed with paperwork.

"It looks like the admiral hangs on to everything."

"This is a huge improvement," she said. "His assistant convinced him to do a monthly sweep to dump the junk. Last month, Josh found a warranty for a Betamax player from 1977."

"I guess it makes sense that Prescott would be in possession of the last remaining copy of the Damascus Cache. It's strange that his office downstairs is so neat."

"You love that office," she said.

"I do. I like to put my feet on the desk and pretend that I'm ruling the world."

"Yeah, well, the people who really rule the world don't operate like that." She crooked a finger at him. "You've got to see this."

"Where are we going?"

"Not far." In the hall, they took a sharp right turn. She pushed open a door, turned on the light and stepped aside so he could enter first. "The office downstairs is just for show. This is where the admiral does his real work."

Chaos reigned. The working office held dozens of cabinets and a huge scarred and battered wooden desk. Every flat surface was covered with papers and weird objects, like model cars and navy caps. The walls were hung with photos; unlike the posed shots downstairs, these were mostly snapshots.

Lexie slipped inside behind him. "I think this represents what's going on inside his head. It looks like a wild jumble, but the admiral knows where everything is. He can walk in the door and lay his hand on whatever he's looking for."

"What did Collier and the CIA guys say when they knew they had to search this room?"

"I wasn't close enough to hear the exact words. Helena told me there were a lot of French curses being thrown around." She gazed directly into his eyes. "An office like this would drive you crazy."

"I like to see the surface of my desk," he admitted. "But there's something I've always wanted to do with an office like this."

"Set fire to it?" she sweetly suggested.

"I'd like to do one of those one-armed sweeps and knock everything onto the floor. Then I'd grab the girl." He suited the action to the word. He cleared a space, took hold of her arm and spun her around. "Then I'd put her on the desk."

He leaned her backward on the wood surface. Though she hadn't resisted him, he saw the fire in her eyes. Her lips pulled back from her teeth.

"That's enough," she snarled.

"Then I'd take off her glasses."

"I don't wear glasses."

"You're beautiful, Lexie." He wasn't playing anymore. Looking down at her, he was struck by a realization so sudden that it had to be true. She was everything he had ever wanted. She was the woman he'd been waiting for. "You're so damn beautiful."

She sat up quickly. "The admiral isn't going to like that you touched his stuff."

"He won't mind when I tell him what I was doing."

"You wouldn't!"

"Don't worry. I'll claim it was an accident. Better yet, I'll blame Collier."

As she stomped from the room, he wondered at her reaction. She liked him, he knew she did. When they were on their date, they were enjoying each other. Why was she constantly pushing him away?

Carrying Helena's computer, Lexie returned to the office and set it down on the counter. After fiddling around on a couple of different sites, she wrote down a six-digit combination to open the safe room. She carefully tucked the note into her pocket and headed for the stairs. "I can't share this with you, Mason."

She wasn't sharing much. The atmosphere between them grew colder and colder. They'd be together for a couple of weeks, at least. There was time enough for him to be patient with her. But he didn't understand. Had he done something to make her mad?

At the door to the safe room, he stayed all the way down the hall so she wouldn't think he was sneaking a peek at the supersecret combination. Carefully, she turned the dial in the middle of the door. When the last tumbler clicked into place, she grabbed the door handle and pulled. The heavy door slowly swung open.

This time, she went first. At the flick of a switch, a cool overhead light came on. The rectangular concrete room was as carefully packed as a shopping boutique. The freestanding wardrobe hangers held several see-through bags, some of gowns and others of fur. Metal lockboxes were stacked on shelves. Three wooden crates marked "Fragile" lined the far wall. Storage racks covered with muslin or plastic held several paintings.

"It's cold," he said.

"The temperature is steady between fifty-five degrees and sixty, which is optimum for the furs. The humidity is set at twenty percent, which is best for the oil paintings."

"If the family ever had to use this room for an extended time, their combined body heat would throw off the storage temp and humidity."

"Here's hoping that Helena never needs to choose between her children and her furs."

He pushed the door closed. A chill intimacy surrounded them. It was just the two of them, tucked away from the rest of the world. Mason had never been a guy who worried about his relationships and dating. But here she was…the girl of his dreams. Getting close to Lexie meant opening himself to the possibility of losing her. She'd made it real clear that she didn't want anything long term.

But he did.

There was trouble ahead. He sensed the impending explosion. The fuse had been lit and the bomb was ticking down to zero hour. He wanted time to duck for cover.

"Is something wrong," he asked, "between you and me?"

"Why? Because I wouldn't have sex with you last night?"

"I wasn't even thinking of that." He paused. It was best to be honest. "Well, yeah, I was thinking about you in bed and how cute you looked in the morning with all those pillows around you. But that's not what I'm talking about. You seem angry."

"I told you before, Mason."

"Got it," he said. "No long-term commitments or relationships. I don't want that, either."

"You don't?"

Now she sounded hurt. He couldn't win! "Are we going to search in here or what?"

She went to the shelves and took down a metal box. Sitting at a small table, she unfastened the latch. Inside, she found an incredible brooch in the shape of a flamingo, a tiara with a huge blue stone, a diamond bracelet and a couple of rings.

When she looked up at him, a tear slipped down her cheek. She quickly dashed it away. "I never thought my life could be like this. I'm juggling diamonds and rubies, and I think the blue one is tanzanite. This is a good job, it pays well and I like the kids. I don't want anything to change."

"Never?"

She carefully returned the jewels to their box. "I'm not going to be a nanny forever. But I'm definitely not leaving a job I really like because some man wants me to."

Not making any sense. She'd gone back to angry.

Now she was referring to him as "some man," and her tone implied that man was a jerk. "Fine."

"You bet it's fine."

He took down a box and opened it. More jewels.

Another was marked "Important Papers." Inside were legal documents, deeds, car titles and other stuff. He sat at the table to sort through it.

Lexie was far from calm. She flipped through the paintings in the storage racks. "I suppose I should take each of these paintings out and feel around the edges for a flash drive."

"Not necessary," he said.

"I want to be thorough."

He placed another metal box on the table and lifted the lid. It was filled with cash—mostly hundreds. With relish, he plunged his hands into it and felt around. "I can see why the Prescotts didn't want the CIA searching down here."

"And not the NSA, either." She went to a wooden crate that was taller than she was. "Should we break these down and see what's inside?"

"I don't think so." He closed the money box and put it on the shelf. "We're done in here."

"Why?"

"Reason number one—the Prescotts aren't deliberately hiding the cache, and this safe room is always closed. Number two—the Damascus Cache is not a flash drive or a microdot."

"Hold on." She waved her arms. "That's what everybody has been looking for, a drive that plugs into a computer."

"Do you think the admiral knows how to use a flash drive?" He asked the rhetorical question and didn't wait for an answer. "From everything I've seen, this is a man who loves documents and disdains technology. If someone wanted to give him a copy of the cache, they'd bring a paper copy of the original."

Her eyes got wide. "You're on to something."

Finally, an acknowledgment. He bowed from the waist. "Thank you, Nancy Drew."

Mason might not be a detective and might not have the right stuff for a long-term relationship, but he was smarter than people expected.

Now he knew what to look for.

Chapter Nineteen

At two o'clock in the afternoon, Grossman and Bertinelli rang the sea chantey doorbell at the Prescott house. Instead of taking them into the cozy kitchen, Lexie escorted them to the huge, sprawling front room with the magnificent furniture that Helena brought to the marriage. There were two Degas paintings on the wall, perfectly maintained and perfectly lit, but the artwork was nothing compared to the view through the arched windows.

This was a breathtaking room; very impressive. She'd purposely brought the NSA agents here so they wouldn't dismiss her as the nanny or a pesky Nancy Drew. She wanted them to take her seriously, and she had learned—by watching Helena—that a display of wealth almost always got respect.

"Gentlemen, please sit. Have some lemonade. Before we get started, I want to set parameters for your search. And I have a few questions."

"This isn't a quid pro quo," Bertinelli said. "You don't get to ask. Our work is classified."

She'd expected a prissy-pants response from him.

For one thing, he didn't like her. For another, he was frustrated by having to answer to Grossman, who was sort of a moron. She smiled and said, "I'd never expect you to betray classified secrets."

She sat on a Scandinavian-style chair beside the sofa. On the coffee table was a tray holding a pitcher of iced lemonade, alongside bowls of strawberries, cream and scones. Though Bertinelli held back, Grossman didn't hesitate before digging in. He sloshed the lemonade on the tray when he poured and loaded a delicate china plate with scones and one strawberry.

"I'm guessing," Grossman said, "there are places the admiral doesn't want us to search. I'm sure he's got private stuff. We all do."

"You have permission to go anywhere," she said, "but Mason and I will accompany you."

Mason came forward and shook hands with both men. Before the NSA agents arrived, she and Mason had decided not to be friendly. He had told her repeatedly that he didn't trust them.

"I should mention," he said, "that the CIA swept for bugs and cameras after their search. And I've gone through the house again. If I find any electronic devices after you leave, I'll have to assume they came from the NSA."

"Why would I bug you?" Grossman asked.

"Doesn't make sense to me," Mason said. "But you boys staked out the house. And you followed us to the restaurant. We must be doing something that you find interesting."

Ignoring the napkin, Grossman wiped his mouth on

the sleeve of his beat-up sweatshirt. With his messy steel-wool hair and sloppy clothes, he was dressed for searching in dark corners of the garage and going through crawl spaces. He looked toward his neatly dressed partner.

"I forget," Grossman said. "Why are we watching them?"

"I thought it was your idea."

Lexie got the sense that Bertinelli was more in charge than the senior agent. She cleared her throat. "The admiral asked me to put together a list of all the people who have been in and out of the house in the past year."

"That's got to be a significant list," Bertinelli said as he finally sat down. "How many names?"

"Over three hundred."

"I want a copy," Bertinelli said.

She pinched her lips together so she wouldn't blurt out what a jerk he was. Why should it be okay for him to get information from her but not the other way around? "Of course, after I get the okay from Admiral Prescott."

"Why do you want it?" Mason asked.

"You never know what might be useful in an investigation," Bertinelli said. "Information is power."

She centered her laptop on the coffee table in front of her. "I'm hoping you can give me details about the people whose photos I'm going to show you. The kind of thing I wouldn't find in a casual search on the internet."

"The dirt," Grossman said. He popped another scone in his mouth.

"I don't mean to gossip," she said.

"Sure you do. When you come right down to it, that's what we do as federal agents. Track down rumors and mine for gossip. Show me the pictures."

She started popping up the pictures on the laptop screen. Mason's computer genius partner had already found ID photos and provided minibiographies. She wanted the gossip. Among all these people, many of whom were tied to the intelligence community, who would have access to the Damascus Cache? Why would they drop it off with the admiral?

Grossman had a lot to say about the handsome Agent Collier, who was sleeping with his supervisor, Margaret Gray, and had bedded three or four other undercover agents.

"Under the cover of his sheets," Grossman said with a laugh.

She'd slipped in Josh Laurent's photo to see if she'd get a reaction. Grossman pointed at the screen. "Isn't that Prescott's assistant?"

She faked surprise. "Oh, you're right. That must have gotten in there by mistake."

"Or maybe not," Bertinelli said. "We've been looking far and wide for suspects. Maybe we should stick to our own backyard. Josh does a lot of whining about why he hasn't been promoted. He's a fan of conspiracy theories."

"Good to know."

It would be ironic if this AC-CD scheme had been engineered by the admiral's pointy-nosed assistant. Josh had the intelligence to create a complicated plot, but she didn't see him as someone who could organize other people. AC-CD was run by a mysterious figure called the leader. Josh? She doubted he could inspire followers.

One of the faces on her laptop belonged to Al Ackerman. Lexie didn't remember him from his visit. The housekeeper had made a note about special food requirements for his Saudi princess bride, but the new wife canceled and didn't make the trip. In her eyes, Al Ackerman became only another one of a group of spies. He had passed away this year.

"Murdered," Grossman said darkly.

She corrected him. "His bio says he died from complications after a heart attack."

"Sure, if those complications included a bullet. Everybody knew Ackerman, especially after he married the princess. In our business, that's dangerous."

Lexie had obtained all the information she wanted from these two agents. She closed up her laptop and resigned herself to spending the rest of the day shepherding Grossman and Bertinelli around the house. No big deal.

She glanced over at Mason and winked. They were handling their investigation like a couple of ace detectives.

AFTER DINNER, MASON followed Lexie into the dramatic front room. It was easy to imagine this house filled with classy, cosmopolitan guests, from Helena's Hollywood contacts to the admiral's acquaintances from the world of international diplomacy. The Prescotts lived large.

Not a lifestyle he envied. Mason didn't need or want all that bustle and noise. The machinations of big money and international business fascinated him, but he was a behind-the-scenes guy. He liked to see how things worked.

He stood behind Lexie by one of the arched windows. Through the glass, a spectacular mountain sunset was unfolding with intense shades of crimson and gold. "So this is how the top one percent lives."

"It is," she said. "I've learned a lot in the past year."

Though he wanted to stroke her shoulders, he kept his hands to himself. "Is this what you want for yourself?"

"No." Her response was fast. "Living like this is way too high maintenance. The best part of the Prescotts' life doesn't have anything to do with money. They're a kind, caring family. And, best of all, Edgar and Helena are truly in love."

He didn't know them well, but he saw signs of their romance throughout the house and also when they were together. "Is that what you're looking for?"

She spun around to face him. "Are you sure I can't go for a walk outside?"

Her lightning-swift change of subject didn't escape him. Lexie would not be drawn into anything resembling a talk about relationships. He answered her question, "Until I'm sure there's no threat aimed at you, you're housebound."

"When will you be sure?"

"The Aspen police haven't found the truck that hit us. Basically, they've got no clue. If my back fender wasn't crumpled, they wouldn't believe it happened."

She paced in front of the window as though trying to simulate a walk in the forest. "Maybe tomorrow?"

"Maybe." There was no need for her to feel trapped. This house was like a very high-class amusement park. He selected the toy he'd most like to play with. "How about a soak in the hot tub?"

She beamed. "You're on."

Upstairs in the giant bedroom, he changed into olive green board shorts. If it had been up to him, he would have gone in the hot tub naked, but he was pretty sure Lexie wouldn't go for it. Before he dashed down to the workout room, he grabbed his shoulder holster. Even though he downplayed the danger, he kept in mind their suspects as well as the person driving the truck. Somebody wanted her dead. It was his job to make sure that didn't happen.

They went downstairs to the gym together. Her coral-colored one-piece bathing suit was just about the sexiest thing he'd ever seen. It wasn't skimpy, but the color was close to her skin tone. When she dropped the towel she'd wrapped around her waist, she appeared to be naked.

He had used this type of hot tub before and got the water started. Before he could play around with adjustments to the temperature, Lexie informed him that the maintenance for the hot tub and the pool was taken care of by the maid service.

A nice perk. There were some things about living large that he could get accustomed to.

The tub was designed for six, so there was plenty of room for him and Lexie to bob around while it filled. It would have been nice to use the lap pool as well, but he understood her concern with wasting water. Drought was a consistent problem in the West. This house had its own well and septic system, but the water table was only so large. Conservation was necessary.

Lexie backed up to a water jet and moaned with pleasure as the water massaged her back. "I can never get enough of this. When I was recovering after the first crash, my dad bought a hot tub. I scolded him about wasting all that money. He laughed and said, 'What makes you think I bought it for you?'"

"Did he use it?"

"Constantly. And so did I."

She ducked her head under the frothy water and then popped up like a cork. She laughed and giggled and splashed as she bounced through the hot liquid. At one point, she burst from the water and darted across the floor to the light switch.

The gym went dark. There was enough glow from the tall windows beside the hot tub and pool to see what they were doing, and he knew when Lexie came back into the water. The great thing about the darkness was being able to look into the forest. The vertical trunks of pine trees formed a backdrop for the leafy thickets and occasional wildflower. Far away, he saw the shadow of the mountains.

"Ackerman," she said.

"What?"

"The guy who married the Saudi princess and was murdered this year. Ackerman. My dad mentioned him."

It was another connection between the past and the present, between the first attack on her and the recent crash. Were they related? He had plenty to think about. For right now, he was content to relax with Lexie and to keep her safe.

Chapter Twenty

Three days had passed, and Lexie hadn't seen anyone but Mason. She'd talked on the phone to other people, but no one had come by the house, and she hadn't been allowed to leave. Not while the truck driver who tried to kill them was still on the loose.

When she considered her enforced alone time with Mason, she should have been bored, but they'd found plenty to do. This house offered a number of amusements. They'd spent time in the gym, watched movies in the theater and taken baths in the hot tub. Last night, she'd baked a pie from scratch. He'd trounced her on all the computer games, and she'd defeated him in chess.

Even more surprising, they hadn't run out of things to talk about. The investigating and her suspect spreadsheet took up some of their conversation, but mostly they talked about themselves, their families and friends, their hopes and dreams. Mason was the most comfortable man she'd ever known, except for one thing.

She missed sex.

He had respected her repeated statement about not wanting a relationship. They could be friends but nothing more. Ha! She wanted a lot more. His muscular body was a constant temptation, and the magnetism was about more than the way he looked. It was his easygoing smile. The way he moved when they did tai chi together. His laughter made her happy, and his rich baritone tickled her desires.

In the middle of the afternoon, she got off the phone in the kitchen and went in search of Mason. He was hanging out in the fancy downstairs office. On the desktop in front of him, he had three framed snapshots that he'd rescued from the chaotic upstairs office.

"Take a look at this," he said. "Here's our suspect, Agent Collier, with his arm around another suspect, his supervisor, whose name is Margaret. They're standing by the fireplace downstairs. I can't tell for sure, but it looks like he's patting her bottom. Grossman thought this was gossip, but they're out front about the attraction."

"That was at a luncheon on New Year's Day," she said. "I was just in the kitchen and—"

"This picture is five agents from NSA. They're a chummy group, but notice this. Bertinelli is glaring at Grossman like he wants to slit his throat."

She really didn't want to talk about suspects. "I had a phone call from Josh."

"One more photo. It's another group scene." He pushed it toward her. "Over on the right side is Ackerman. It looks like he's presenting something to the admiral. Can you tell what it is?"

She peered at the photo. "It's an Arabian vase made

of brass that looks like Aladdin's lamp, only it's bigger and taller. I know exactly where it is."

He glanced up at her. His eyes were an unreal shade of blue. His lips moved and her attention shifted to his mouth. She heard him say, "Why do you know where the vase is?"

"I made it disappear." As she spoke, she gathered her self-control so she wouldn't fly across the desk and attach herself to him like a limpet on steroids. "The admiral had it downstairs in a place of honor because it was a gift from his buddy and the princess. Helena hated it. I've got to say, I'm on Helena's side. The vase is cheesy. She asked me to get it out of her sight. So I moved it to the admiral's office."

"Then it's nothing important?"

"Probably not."

Mason shrugged. "Did you say something about a phone call?"

"It was Josh. He told me that Helena was stopping by the outdoor camp in Oregon to check on Stella."

"What's wrong with the munchkin?"

"She's feeling sick," she said. "Then Josh told me that he's coming back to Aspen and staying at the house. His arrival is tomorrow at eleven thirty."

Mason's grin faltered. "We won't have the place to ourselves anymore."

She hadn't been planning to make a decision so quickly. For the past three nights, she'd spent many sleepless hours on her side of the pillows, trying to make up her mind. But now it hit her: a sudden, certain revelation. Nothing had ever been so clear. They needed to have sex before the house was invaded by Josh and others. They needed to have sex now.

She reached across the desk and took his hand. Her voice dropped to a husky whisper. "We should take advantage of our time alone. There's not much left. Come upstairs and help me move some pillows."

He vaulted out from behind the desk. "It's about time." He pulled her out to the hallway and into the foyer. "I've been obsessed with your pillow wall. I want to destroy it." He started on the staircase, taking two at a time. When she couldn't keep up, he yanked her off her feet and carried her. "Let's set all these damn pillows on fire."

He dropped her in the middle of the bed.

She grabbed a pillow with each hand and flung them onto the floor. "Down, wall, down."

Leaping up beside her, he got rid of more pillows.

In seconds the bed was cleared. They were standing on top of the mattress where famous people had slept, staring at each other and breathing hard. Mason unclipped his holster from his belt and carefully placed the gun on the bedside table. With an evil grin, he turned toward her. He lunged and tackled her and they crashed down together.

Lexie was not inexperienced when it came to sex, but Mason's kisses made her feel as if this were the first time. He was so eager, nearly desperate. His mouth was everywhere. His hands roamed wildly over her body. And she was the same way, unbuckling his belt and groping until she touched his hard erection. Her self-imposed drought was over. *Let it rain.*

Gradually, they slowed to a less frantic, more sensual pace. His long fingers combed her hair back from her face until he reached her ponytail. With a deft twist, he unfastened the band she used to hold her hair back.

Her curls tumbled free, and he paused, rising over her on the bed and gazing down. "You're a beautiful woman, Lexie."

How could she respond to that? To say yes would be arrogant. No was a sure indication of poor self-esteem.

"Same to you," she said. "I mean, not a woman. And *beautiful* probably isn't the right word."

"I know what you mean."

"I thought you might."

They had much in common, but they weren't a perfect fit. And there were still reasons why they shouldn't take this relationship to the next level. But she wasn't going to stop.

She stroked down his chest to the edge of his T-shirt, and then she slipped her hand under the fabric and pulled it up, baring his torso and his rock-hard abs. She stroked and fondled and tweaked, and before she knew it, his shirt was off.

When she got dressed this morning, she hadn't consciously thought about having sex, but she'd worn the perfect outfit for a simple strip: a striped blue blouse with buttons and a front-fastening bra.

He pushed her back on the bed and went to work on the buttons. In a few practiced moves, he had unhooked her bra and pushed the flimsy lace aside. Slowly, he lowered his head and suckled at her breasts. With every lash of his tongue against her tight nipples, an electric surge shot through her body.

"The rest of these clothes need to be gone," she said. "Right now."

"You think?"

She looked down the length of his body. His belt was unfastened and his jeans were pushed down to show a glimpse of black jersey boxers and a very large bulge. Farther down… "You still have your boots on."

"And an ankle holster."

Going to bed with an armed man was never a good idea. Was this a warning? Was she making a big mistake?

Removing the rest of their clothing wasn't graceful, but when their bodies came together, she felt as beautiful as he'd said she was. Having sex with Mason felt like a dance with different rhythms and textures than she'd ever felt before. Smoothly, he guided her through the steps, and she was happy to let him lead, right up until the moment when he rose above her and parted her thighs.

"Wait," he whispered.

She knew what was coming, knew what he would say. She knew she wasn't going to like this. Still, she asked, "Why?"

"I have a condom in my wallet."

She didn't need one, would never need one again. There were other health protection reasons, but she never needed to worry about getting pregnant. She stiffened in anger. The dance was over. Reality had intruded.

Though he had been ready to mount her, he had

changed positions. On the bed beside her, he cuddled her against his chest as though he could protect her by absorbing her sadness and rage.

"Something's wrong," he said.

"I'm okay."

She'd come this far and it had been amazing. She refused to turn around and go back, not even if she was leading him into a lie. Couldn't she pretend, just for a moment, that they were a normal couple? Couldn't she have this pleasure, just a thin slice of happiness to cut through the darkness?

She turned so she was facing him. It wasn't a lie. As long as she didn't do something stupid and tell him that she loved him, she wasn't making a promise.

Her frustration channeled into passion. As she threw herself into sex, every muscle in her body tensed. Her breasts flattened against his chest. She clenched her legs around him.

"Easy, now," he whispered.

"I don't want to go easy."

But he was much stronger, and he was in total control. He soothed her, cajoled her with slow caresses. So patient, so sweet, he entered her slowly, almost cautiously, as though she might shatter. His kisses were soft and gentle as he eased into a simple tempo.

Again, she was trembling. Goose bumps prickled her arms. This time, the earthquake that rattled her body came from pure satisfaction and relief. When she fell back onto the bed, her smile was real.

A happy sound—sort of like a meow—came through her lips. It wasn't anything she'd heard from herself before. "You know, Mason, I wouldn't mind having a pillow."

"Only one," he said.

He pulled up a pillow, set it against the headboard and arranged the duvet so they could lie comfortably in each other's arms. In this cozy position, with an orgasm still resonating inside her, she wondered why on earth she kept pushing him away.

"It'd be nice to have servants," she said.

"Is there something you want?"

"Dinner."

The cook had left the freezer filled with prepared meals that only needed to be microwaved to be ready, but Lexie felt too blissfully lazy to even turn the microwave dial. She hadn't been so utterly relaxed in ages.

There was a noise from downstairs. Mason heard it, too. In two seconds, he pulled on his black boxers, grabbed his gun and went to the door. He eased it open and slipped into the hallway.

She fumbled from one side of the huge bed to the other, trying to find her clothes. She didn't hear gunfire from downstairs. *A good sign.*

She'd just zipped her jeans when the bedroom door flew open and Stella dashed inside. Lexie managed to get two buttons fastened before she wrapped her arms around the little girl and scooped her off the floor.

"Hey, cutie pie. What are you doing here?"

Stella poked out her lower lip. "I'm sick."

Helena charged through the door with Mason following. "I don't know what she has, but I wanted her to see her regular doctor, so I pulled her out of camp."

Lexie nodded. "Okay."

Stella pointed at Mason and giggled. "He's got no shirt."

"Pretty funny," Lexie said.

"Hysterical," Helena said as she glanced between them. Lexie wasn't sure if her boss approved or disapproved. Probably the latter.

Stella hopped down and went toward the messy bed. "Lexie, were you taking a nap?"

"You caught me."

"I don't like naps," Stella said as she meandered around the room. "I'm too old for nap time. Lexie, does Mason take naps with you?"

She swallowed hard. This would be complicated to explain.

"Let me," Helena said as she made a dramatic swoop toward her daughter. "Sometimes, when a boy and a girl like each other a great deal, they sleep together."

"In the middle of the day?" Stella wrinkled her nose at the ridiculous idea.

"And at night, too."

Helena cast a radiant smile at all of them. The actress actually believed that her quick thinking had averted the crisis, and she wouldn't have to explain to Stella in more detail. Lexie knew better. This little girl asked question after question. She wouldn't give up so easily.

Hoping to create a diversion, Lexie charged through the bedroom door into the hallway. "Let's bring your luggage inside."

Standing behind Lexie at the top of the staircase, Stella asked, "Lexie, do you like Mason?"

"Sure I do."

"Do you love him? Are you going to marry him?"

And there they were: the two sentences she wanted most to avoid. Sometimes she just couldn't catch a break.

Chapter Twenty-One

The explanations to Helena weren't difficult. While Lexie thawed dinner, tossed a salad and chatted to Stella, who was playing in the family room, Mason told Helena about the threats to the house and possibly to Lexie.

"The only way I could be sure she was safe all night was to sleep in the same room," he said. "That's why we took the larger suite."

Helena nodded and sipped the vodka martini with two olives that he'd made for her. Mason and Lexie weren't drinking.

"I'm too tall for the sofa," he said. "Lexie graciously allowed me to join her in the bed. She set up a wall of pillows between us."

"Then the wall came tumbling down," Helena said. "It's all right, Mason. If the other children were here, we might have to come up with another explanation so we wouldn't give the impression that we approve of or condone premarital relationships. The older boys would be quick to use that as ammunition when they bring girls home."

He remembered what it was like to be a teenage boy. Eddy Jr. was nearly ready to start driving. The twins were sneaking up on puberty. He didn't envy the situations Helena and the admiral would soon face. "Stella seems to accept that Lexie and I like each other and take naps together."

Helena cast a worried glanced in her daughter's direction. "She was running a temperature yesterday. When it continued into today, I felt like she needed to see the doctor. Stella is usually such a healthy child."

In the family room, the little princess sat at a kid-size table and colored in a book about Cinderella. Lexie peeked over her shoulder. Subtly, she felt Stella's forehead and frowned.

"What did your doc say?" Lexie asked.

"His office is running tests. If she's all right, I'll take her back to camp tomorrow. If not, she'll have to stay here." She confronted him directly. "Is this threat real?"

"As real as the dent in my bumper."

"We'll need to find somewhere else for Stella to stay. And for Lexie, as well. I had no idea how dangerous this was."

"We'll be all right tonight," he said firmly. "I'll contact my office and have another two guards sent for tomorrow."

She finished off her martini and asked for another. In his brief acquaintance with Helena, he hadn't seen her as a drinker. This was a different side of the actress's personality. She seemed a hundred times more subdued. Her voice was deeper. She looked tired.

That night in their bedroom, he asked Lexie about the change in Helena. "Is this a case of maternal concern?"

Lexie stuck her head through the open door and looked down the hallway toward the Prescotts' suite, where Helena would be sharing her bed with her youngest daughter. Talking in a low voice, Lexie said, "Yes, she's worried about Stella. Helena is a busy woman with her fingers in a lot of pies, but the kids are important to her. She told me that the drinking and the bummed-out mood are for the role she's playing. She's also trying to drop ten pounds in three days."

"By drinking martinis?"

"I don't ask," Lexie said.

She threw back the duvet and got into bed wearing one of her child-appropriate nightshirts. This one had row upon row of flamingos. She had left the door to their bedroom open so he could hear any disturbance and do his bodyguard thing.

His gaze devoured her. "How am I going to lie beside you and not make love?"

"Helena locked the door to her suite. Maybe they won't hear us."

Their first act of passion had been loud and energetic, involving the throwing of pillows and moans of pleasure and tackling and grabbing. The memory made him smile broadly. "We might be able to tone it down."

"Stella is only six. But I think she'll know the difference between napping and what we were doing before."

"I'm going to take that as a challenge. Silent sex." Now that he'd had a taste of the incredible passion that had been growing between them, he wasn't going to stop. "Aren't there religious sects that do that?"

"We can try."

That was all he needed to hear. They would be very quiet and very, very hot.

THE NEXT MORNING, Lexie was annoyed to find Josh standing at the front door before nine o'clock. He pushed a pair of horn-rimmed glasses up his nose and gave her a terse smile. "I caught an earlier flight."

"I didn't know you wore glasses."

"There wasn't time this morning to put in my contacts." He dragged his suitcase across the threshold. "Did Helena get here with Stella?"

"I didn't know she was coming yesterday," Lexie said. "A heads-up would have been nice."

"When I talked to her she hadn't made firm plans about pulling Stella out of camp. I hope she didn't catch you in the middle of a wild party or anything."

You little beaky pervert! That was exactly what he'd been hoping—that Lexie would get caught. She'd come within minutes of having that be true. Helena wasn't upset now, but if she'd walked in on them while they were… It would have been bad.

"Where are you going to sleep?" she asked him.

"If Helena stays, I'll take the basement."

There was a small, plain, windowless bedroom in the basement near the safe room. Josh preferred it to the second- and third-floor guest rooms when the kids were at the house, because he liked the privacy. She'd never asked why he needed to be private, just assumed it was something creepy.

"Put your suitcase in the hall closet," she said. "We'll figure it out later. Right now I need to get breakfast."

In the kitchen, Mason sat at the counter. He saluted their entrance with a mug of coffee, which she figured must be his second, because he seemed wide awake.

"Good to see you, Josh. How are things at the Pentagon?"

"Every time the admiral goes there, he gets pulled into more meetings, totally unrelated to his main concerns. Our only solid information on the Damascus Cache is that all copies were destroyed years ago in a computer purge."

Mason exchanged a look with her. "What if there was a hard copy?"

"On paper? Nope, no way." Josh had noticed their sly glance. His head swiveled like a woodpecker's as he looked from her to Mason and back again. "What did you find out?"

"We were speculating," Mason said. "We didn't locate the cache. Neither did a team from the CIA or two agents from NSA."

Wrapped in a silky robe, Helena joined them, pouring herself a mug of coffee. "Stella's still running a fever. I thought I'd let her stay in bed as long as possible."

"Good plan," Lexie said.

Since they were all at the counter, she decided to do breakfast like a short-order cook, with a menu of any-style eggs, toast and bacon. Helena and Mason both wanted scrambled with cheese melted on top. Josh wanted over easy, which meant he'd get served last.

Josh pointed to the chart on the flat screen on the wall in the family room. "What's that?"

Lexie winced. She hadn't changed the screen back to the usual display of family schedules. "It's a spreadsheet for suspects."

Mason took over the explanation, detailing that these were all the people who had been through the house and why they were there.

"Amazing," Helena said. "I didn't realize we did so much entertaining."

"Why is my name up there?" Josh asked. "Am I a suspect?"

Lexie wanted to tell him that he was their number one suspicious person and would, no doubt, spend the rest of his miserable, pointy-nosed life in a federal prison cell. But she opted for honesty. "We're just being thorough."

"I'm impressed," he said. "Can you run me off a copy?"

"I'll send the list to your email."

"Me, too," Helena said. "What else have you been doing?"

While Lexie served them breakfast and made up a plate for herself, Mason used the remote control to scroll through photos of their various suspects. Every time Helena made a comment, he slowed to study the person. He paused on Ackerman.

Helena exhaled a melodramatic sigh. "That poor,

sad man. Lexie, do you remember that dreadful vase he gave us?"

"I made it disappear into the admiral's upstairs office."

"Perfect. Ackerman wanted Edgar to have it. And I don't have to look at it."

She also had a comment for Collier. "A ladies' man. He has women crawling all over him."

Josh finished eating, shoved his empty plate toward Lexie and dashed to the front closet, where he'd left his computer along with his suitcase. He returned to the kitchen, laptop in hand. "I'll need all this information. All the photos."

"Not so fast," she said, remembering her conversation with Bertinelli. "Let's try a bit of quid pro quo. What have you got that I might find interesting?"

"This isn't a game," he said with a haughty air of entitlement. "You should give the information to someone who can use it."

"And I could say the same to you."

"Fine." He tapped a few keys on his computer. "I just sent you a couple of my files. One of them is a brochure for AC-CD."

She really didn't care what it was. She just wanted to win. If this international incident involving the Damascus Cache was going to be solved because of work she and Mason had done, she wanted credit. Maybe even a raise. Maybe she should have a change in status. She could be a nanny/investigator.

Chapter Twenty-Two

While Josh stormed off to parts unknown in the huge house, Helena's cell phone rang. She squinted at the caller identification. "It's the doctor's office."

Helena strode away from the counter, holding the phone to her ear, and Lexie looked toward Mason. "Multiply this by six kids and you have a typical morning at the Prescott home."

"With one major difference," he said. "All the kids are more mature than Josh. He's so damn whiny."

"He's supposed to be real smart," she said, "but you and I were the ones who made up the spreadsheet of suspects."

Mason took out his phone—which was synced with hers—and pulled up the files that Josh had transferred. "He's got basically nothing here. Places where AC-CD has been active, members of the group who are in prison. Here's their brochure."

He held his phone so she could read the sheet that was put together in a simple format. The first thing that struck her eye was the motto under the logo for Anti-Conspiracy Committee for Democracy: Information Is Power. It was attributed to Thomas Jefferson, but she'd heard the words recently. "Did you see this? That's what Bertinelli said."

"He could be the AC-CD leader," Mason said. "Under his snotty, obsessive-compulsive exterior, he's a smart guy."

Had he been purposely giving them a clue? Or was he setting Lexie and Mason up to look foolish? "I don't like these games of one-upmanship. Why can't people just say what they mean?"

"Everybody lies," he said.

"Is that something you learned in international studies?"

"As a matter of fact, it is. But I also learned it in life."

"How?"

"Whether it's a fib about remembering somebody's name or a fake alibi for murder, we all dabble in misdirection. Even you."

She couldn't argue.

WHEN HELENA STRODE back into the room, her eyes were red-rimmed and bloodshot. Mason thought she'd been crying, but he couldn't be sure that she wasn't practicing for her upcoming role. The actress was hard to read.

"I'm a terrible mother," she said.

"You're not," Lexie said as she hugged Helena tightly. "What did the doctor say?"

"My darling little Stella has a strange variety of measles that's running rampant in Europe. She must have been exposed when we were in New York for a fashion show."

"Is it serious?" Lexie asked.

"No, she's been vaccinated so the case will be mild, and the doctor will contact the pharmacy and have meds delivered. He gave me the okay to leave." She gave a loud sob. "When I heard the doctor say that, I was relieved. That's why I'm a bad mother. I was glad that I didn't have to worry about my child and I could carry on with this movie role."

"That doesn't make you bad," Lexie said.

"I should cancel the movie."

While Lexie escorted Helena into the family room and they put their heads together, he had his own re-action to the news. If Stella had measles, the family surely wouldn't want Lexie to take care of her. He'd al-ways heard that young women were supposed to avoid measles, mumps and rubella. She'd probably already been vaccinated, but he wanted to know for sure. Be-fore he could pry her away from Helena, the house alarm went off. It gave one blast, then another, and then it went silent.

He ripped his gun from the holster and dashed to the foyer entrance. Inside the code box that disarmed the alarm was a schematic. He checked the blinking light. The alarm had originated from downstairs—from the door near the safe room.

Lexie and Helena appeared in the foyer. "Upstairs," he ordered them. "Make sure Stella is okay. Stay in Helena's room. Door locked."

He raced down the staircase.

Josh was coming down the hall toward him, waving both hands in front of his face. "Sorry, sorry, I set it off by accident."

Mason didn't put his gun away. "Why did you open that door?"

"I wanted to go outside and catch my breath. Lexie got me all flustered with her quid pro quo. I forgot the code for a moment, but then I remembered."

"I'll be making a thorough search of the house." Mason watched Josh to see if he had a guilty reaction. There was nothing. "I need to be certain we're secure."

"Like I said, sorry."

Mason pivoted and ran upstairs to tell the ladies that all was clear and Josh was an idiot. At the door to the Prescotts' suite, he tapped on the door. Helena opened it.

"False alarm," he said. "Josh wanted to go outside and accidentally set it off."

"I don't know which is more incredible—Josh being outside or Josh being sloppy enough to forget the code."

Beyond her shoulder, he saw Stella leaping across the bed toward Lexie. The kid didn't look sick at all. He waved to her. "Hey, princess."

"Mason is a basin," she yelled to him.

"Stelly is made of jelly."

"I'm not Stelly."

"Grant me some poetic license, kiddo. You're sweet like jelly."

She flopped on the bed. "Okay."

He took Lexie's hand and directed her away from the room and the germs in it. "We need to talk. Ladies, will you excuse us?"

As soon as they were in the hall, she asked, "What's wrong?"

He took her into their bedroom, closed and locked the door. "Stella has measles. I'm not sure what happens with the variety she has. According to Helena, it's some new variety from Europe. In any case, you should check it out before you expose yourself."

She shook her head. "I don't understand."

"This might be an old wives' tale, but I heard verification when we studied international pandemics in college. Measles can cause infertility in adults."

Realization hit her like a splash of cold water to the face. She gasped. Then she burst into tears. Her legs crumpled and she was on the floor, sobbing.

"I'm sure you're okay," he said. "We can go to the doctor right now."

"It doesn't matter."

"If it didn't you wouldn't be so upset."

She raised her tearstained face. "Fertility isn't an issue for me. After my first car crash, I had a hysterectomy. Mason, I can't have children."

"Then we don't have to worry about exposure."

"Did you hear what I said? I will never have kids. If you and I have a relationship, it'll never be what you want. I can't give you a family."

"I don't care."

"But I do."

LEXIE FLED FROM the bedroom and rushed down the staircase, not knowing where she was going. Her world was falling apart. She'd finally found the right guy, the man her dad would have wanted her to settle down and raise a family with. Mason was a partner, a friend and the best lover she'd ever known. He deserved children.

In the foyer, she blindly lurched toward the lower level. She needed to be alone, locked in the safe room where no one could hear her sobs. Could she remember that combination from yesterday? Doubtful. Instead, she went into the movie theater—the room the admiral had made soundproof and invisible to electronic searches.

She flung the door open and ran inside. The curtained room resembled an actual theater with well-padded seats that had footrests and separate snack tables. Four risers went all the way to the back wall. At the front there was a stage the kids used for performances. There were two screens, one that lowered and one huge flat screen.

She spotted Josh's head in one of the front row seats. He was just sitting there, motionless and in the way.

"Get out!"

He didn't move.

"Get out, get out, get out."

She ran toward him, ready to forcibly eject him if necessary. She wanted privacy for her breakdown. When she stood in front of him, she stopped. The handle of a hunting knife protruded from Josh's scrawny chest. The front of his shirt was covered in blood.

"Hello, Franny."

She whirled at the sound of his voice. "Anton Karpov."

"I go by Tony now—Tony Curtis, like the actor." He held his hands wide, gesturing to the stage he stood on. In his right hand, he had a Glock. "And you go by Lexie."

"Why are you here? How did you get in?"

"You can figure it out. You always were a smarty-pants. One plus one."

"Josh let you in."

She noticed the blood on the sleeve of his denim jacket. "Why did you kill him?"

"He's not dead, not yet. Wiggle your fingers, Josh. Show her that you're okay."

She noticed the slightest bit of movement. "He's lost a lot of blood. We have to get him to a hospital."

"Not until he gives me what I want." He strode across the stage as though he were lecturing her, schooling her on how to be a violent psychopath. "Our little Josh found the Damascus Cache. And the first thing he did was call the leader of AC-CD and tell him. It seems Josh has been blackmailing our leader for quite some time, and he forgot how to show the proper respect, the proper amount of fear."

Was it only a year ago that she'd dated Anton? How could she have been so blind? Yes, he was good-looking, with his blue eyes and his thick Tony Curtis hair. But his inner ugliness made him grotesque.

At the time, she hadn't thought she could do better than Anton, hadn't thought she deserved better. Mason had shown her a different way. He could care about her. But there was no future for them.

Anton said, "As soon as Josh gives me the cache, I'm gone. And you can take him to a hospital. What do you say, Josh? Do you want to live?"

His lips twitched. "Vase."

"I know what he's talking about." The Arabian vase from Ackerman, hidden in the admiral's office. "I know where it is. Should I take you there?"

"As soon as I get within karate range, you'll attack."

It was gratifying to know that he was still scared of her, but it was inconvenient. "Then you have to let me go and get it."

"So you can bring reinforcements? I don't think so."

"Rock and a hard place, Anton. What are you going to do?"

Muttering to himself, he paced back and forth on the stage. She watched him carefully, measuring his stride, plotting a possible move. If he hadn't been armed, she could have taken him. But she knew Anton, and he was an ace marksman.

"I should have killed you before," he said.

"Were you driving the truck that smashed Mason's fender?"

His smile was ice-cold. "That was my second try at vehicular homicide. The first time, I was in a black car, and you were on the road near Buena Vista. In that little bronze sedan you crashed off the cliff."

Her heart stopped. "You're lying."

"It was me, Franny. I've been working for the leader for years. He was disappointed that you didn't die." He bent at the waist and stared at her. "When you think about it, I did you a favor. The person you really want to hurt is the leader."

"Sam Bertinelli," she said. Bertinelli had quoted the motto of AC-CD. He had been spying on her. He was stronger and smarter than he acted while hiding behind his junior agent pose.

"Good guess," Anton said. "But not a smart guess. I want Bertinelli to keep paying for these jobs, and if you accuse him, he'll be out of business."

He lowered his gun and took aim. "I'm afraid you're going to have to die."

"No way, psycho."

She dived across the row of chairs and flattened herself on the floor while he fired three shots. She heard him moving and dodged to a different place. He fired again.

Her hope was that Mason would hear the gunfire. Not even the best soundproofing could muffle the concussive explosion of a bullet being fired, which was why Anton had used a knife on Josh.

Reaching the top row, she ducked underneath the risers. And there it was. The brass vase holding the Damascus Cache was right there on the floor at the back of the room. She wouldn't let Anton have it.

He dropped to the floor opposite her. His hard, cruel eyes peered through the scaffolding under the risers. "I see you, Franny."

She vaulted up and onto the risers again. Holding the handle of the brass vase, she dashed across the row of seats.

He'd taken too long to climb back up. She was close enough to fight him. Her flying kick hit him in the arm, but he didn't lose his gun.

She heard the door to the room open. Mason stood there, aiming his weapon with both hands. "Drop it."

She looked down at Anton. "Do as he says."

When he hesitated, she swung hard with the vase and connected with the side of his skull. Anton hit the floor, unconscious.

Mason had her in his arms. "Are you okay?" He kissed her forehead. "Were you shot?" Another kiss and another.

"I'm okay. But Josh is at death's door. We should call 911."

"Already did. As soon as I heard gunfire, I told Helena to get the cops and the EMTs."

"How did you know we'd need an ambulance?"

"I know you, Lexie." He smoothed the hair off her forehead. "If there's ever a confrontation, you'll kick somebody's butt hard enough that they need a doctor."

"I guess that's true."

"It's one of the things that make you special. I love you, Lexie."

"I'm not the right woman for you, remember? We can be friends, maybe even lovers. But we can't ever have a family."

He took his wallet from his pocket. "Have I ever shown you a picture of my brother?"

She took the official Marine Corps photograph from him. His brother was handsome in his uniform and his cap. "He's African-American."

"We were adopted, both of us. That was the family I grew up in, and it's the kind of family I want."

She knew how much he adored his brother. Adopted? "You don't care if the kids aren't your own?"

"But they are," he said. "If I raise them, they're my

kids. I'm their dad. You're their mom. You don't need to have a baby to be a good mother."

She held him close. "I love you, Mason. And I always will."

"Let's clean up these scumbags and get out of here."

"Were you planning to go somewhere?"

He picked up the brass vase. "I think our first stop should be the Pentagon, where we can drop this off with the admiral. And maybe we'll drop off Stella, as well."

"What about us?"

He suggested an elopement followed by a honeymoon in Paris, but she wanted her dad to meet the man she married before the ceremony. They were off to Texas and on their way to happily ever after.

* * * * *

"Paige?" Jax whispered.

He could have sworn everything stopped. His heartbeat. His breath. Maybe even time. But that standstill didn't last.

Because the person stepped out, not enough for him to fully see her, but Jax knew it was a woman.

"You got my message," she said. "I'm so sorry."

Paige. It was her. In the flesh.

Jax had a thousand emotions hit him at once. Relief. Mercy, there was a ton of relief, but it didn't last but a second or two before the other emotions took over: shock, disbelief and, yeah, anger.

Lots and lots of anger.

"Why?" he managed to say, though he wasn't sure how he could even speak with his throat clamped shut.

Paige cleared her throat, too. "Because it was necessary."

As answers went, it sucked, and he let her know that with the scowl he aimed at her. "Why?" he repeated.

She stepped from the shadows but didn't come closer to him. Still, it was close enough for him to confirm what he already knew.

This was Paige.

She was back from the grave. Or else back from a lie that she'd apparently let him believe.

For a *dead* woman, she didn't look bad, but she had changed. No more blond hair. It was dark brown now and cut short and choppy. She'd also lost some of those curves that'd always caught his eye and every other man's in town.

"I know you have a thousand questions," she said, rubbing her hands along the outside legs of her jeans. She also glanced around. Behind him.

Behind her.

"Just one question. Why the hell did you let me believe you were dead?"

Don't miss SIX-GUN SHOWDOWN
by USA TODAY *bestselling author Delores Fossen,*
available in August 2016 wherever
Harlequin® Intrigue books and ebooks are sold.

www.Harlequin.com

Reading Has Its Rewards

Earn **FREE BOOKS!**

Register at **Harlequin My Rewards** and submit your Harlequin purchases from wherever you shop to earn points for free books and other exclusive rewards.

Plus submit your purchases from now till May 30th for a chance to win a $500 Visa Card*.

Visit **HarlequinMyRewards.com** today

MYR16R1

Love the Harlequin book you just read?

Your opinion matters.

Review this book on your favorite book site, review site, blog or your own social media properties and share your opinion with other readers!

HARLEQUIN®

A *Romance* FOR EVERY MOOD™

JUST CAN'T GET ENOUGH?

Join our social communities
and talk to us online.

You will have access to the latest
news on upcoming titles and special
promotions, but most importantly,
you can talk to other fans about your
favorite Harlequin reads.

Harlequin.com/Community

 Facebook.com/HarlequinBooks

 Twitter.com/HarlequinBooks

 Pinterest.com/HarlequinBooks

THE WORLD IS BETTER
WITH
Romance

Harlequin has everything from contemporary, passionate and heartwarming to suspenseful and inspirational stories.

Whatever your mood,
we have a romance just for you!

Connect with us to find your next great read, special offers and more.